ROGUE PATRIOT

© 2016 Mike Trial
www.miketrialwriter.com

ISBN: 978-1-942168-49-2 Paperback
ISBN: 978-1-942168-48-5 eBook

All rights reserved. No part of this book may be reproduced or transmitted in any form or by any means, electronic or mechanical or by any information or storage and retrieval system without permission in writing from the author or publisher.

Published by Compass Flower Press
an imprint of AKA-Publishing
Columbia. Missouri

www.AKA-Publishing.com

ROGUE PATRIOT

MIKE TRIAL

CHAPTER 1

Rear Admiral Richardson, Chief of Naval Intelligence Western Pacific, put a map projection on the big screen that covered one wall of the crowded Operations Center. He zoomed down to northeastern North Korea. "These are intelligence satellite images—three hours old," Richardson said. His red laser indicator touched a railcar on a siding. "Last night, the North Korean Strategic Rocket Forces moved their one fully operational ballistic missile to this launch facility." He zoomed in until the image pixelated then backed out to focus on the three missile stages on their railcars, and a pile of gray tarpaulins beside the tracks.

Richardson turned to the twenty people at the semi-circular table facing the screen. "I reiterate, this is TOP SECRET, need to know," his eyes stopped at one of two civilians in the room—a small man, fit, well dressed—and attentive.

"He stays," Admiral William Hallam, the senior officer in the room, and Chief of U.S. Naval Forces Western Pacific said softly. "He's cleared and we need everyone's input on this situation."

J.D. Iselin, CEO of Iselin Security Options, turned to Admiral Hallam. "Your SEALS' training with our Ghost drones is complete, you may not need me at this point."

Hallam stopped him. "No, you stay, JD. He turned to Rear Admiral Richardson. "Proceed."

"The National Reconnaissance Office has put a Global Hawk on loiter to track the launch site continuously." A crystal clear overhead picture came onto the projection. "Tae Po Dong 2, three stage, liquid fueled, ballistic missile," he said. "North Korea's most advanced."

"We're sure it's not a decoy?" someone asked.

"We're sure. This rail car originated at their high security missile manufacturing site and was brought directly to the launch site."

"That's unusual," someone added. "They usually run the railcars around some so we don't see the direct route..."

"This time they're in a hurry to launch," Richardson said. He put a large red circle on the map, centered on the launch site. The circle took in all of Japan, Taiwan, Guam, North China, and Eastern Siberia. "That missile is capable of putting a twenty-kiloton warhead on target anywhere in this circle."

Richardson zoomed back into the launch site and indicated a wisp of steam at tankage on the north side of the launch platform. "They have already delivered liquid oxygen to the site." The red dot of his pointer touched a mobile crane. "They're now moving up the mobile crane they'll use to stack the missile. After stacking, fueling will take four hours, during which time they will place the warhead and set its guidance."

"Total time from now until they can launch?" Hallam asked.

"No more than ten hours."

There was much rustling around the table. Richardson shifted.

"Relax, you are the messenger, not the enemy," Hallam said to Richardson. "Turn up the room lights."

In the suddenly over-bright room, a Vice Admiral with sea-operations tabs on his uniform addressed Hallam, "Sir, they know our satellites are seeing this. In the past, prior to putting a missile on the pad, there was a pronouncement from the Kim government about 'peaceful use of space' by the People's Republic of North Korea. As of now there has been nothing."

An Air Force colonel on his left added, "And there is nothing in the regional situation to provoke Kim Jong-un into making a gesture."

"They don't have much fuel manufacturing and storage capability," the Vice Admiral said. "If they've brought kerosene and liquid oxygen to the site, they're going to launch."

"Maybe Kim Jong-un himself doesn't know about this," said Richardson.

"Possibly," Hallam agreed equably. "Elaborate."

Richardson turned to a small, bald-headed man dressed in open collar shirt and sports jacket. "I think perhaps Mr. Kyle can speak to that."

The CIA Japan/Korea bureau chief stood. "The most obvious candidate for this level of insubordination in the Kim regime is General Chae. There should be a photo..." A photo of a Korean in an impeccable blue uniform with Strategic Rocket Forces insignia on the shoulder boards came on the screen. Unlike most Koreans, he had grey eyes.

Richardson added, "The Strategic Rocket Forces are an army branch, like armor, infantry, or artillery, but it is also a government directorate that includes special weapons development, like nuclear weapons. A Mr. Park is the chief scientist..."

"Mr. Park is chief scientist," Kyle interjected. "But he's not in the line of military authority. Interestingly, Park was educated here in Japan in the post WWII years."

"Stay on task, Mr. Kyle," Hallam said.

"Yes sir," Kyle said. "Chae's family got him his position through patronage. But he is highly intelligent, a good leader, very aggressive, and an ultranationalist, the scion of one of the most prestigious old-line Korean families. His family is wealthy. He's travelled overseas, so he knows what the world is like. He sees North Korea falling further and further behind other nations, especially China. His family aligned with the Japanese during WWII and lost a great deal when the Chinese took back Manchuria."

"So Chae doesn't hate the U.S.A. or Japan so much as he hates China," Hallam mused. "Enough to launch a single nuclear strike against China?"

"No, sir," Richardson said. "He knows that would simply provoke China into launching an invasion of North Korea, which they would win."

"And our agency believes if that happens," Kyle added, "The Red Army would continue their march south and take South Korea. We could not stop them."

"All right, let me summarize. We need to develop an operations plan," Hallam said. "This missile preparation appears to be without the Kim government's approval, or even knowledge. It will likely not be a strike against China. So that leaves either a demonstration launch or a strike against Japan or South Korea."

"Taking out Busan, South Korea with a nuclear weapon, then invading from the North would be a pretty good strategy," the Air Force Colonel said.

Hallam turned to his chief of staff.

"What have we heard from CINCPACFLT in Hawaii?"

"A rather ominous silence, sir."

Hallam turned back to the men and women at the table. "Then I need a tactical plan, right now."

"We don't believe this launch is empty posturing," Kyle added. "He's done over-flights of Japan. This will be a real strike."

"What's the official word from Seoul and Tokyo?" Hallam asked.

The South Korean liaison colonel stood. "My

government has activated our Hyunmu 2C anti-ballistic missile forces. The semi-tractor trailers that launch the missiles are spreading out across the highway network now." He sat down.

The Japan Self Defense Force colonel stood up. "Sir," he said in perfect California English, "My government is moving two anti-missile cruisers to point C. The screen operator moved the screen to a large-scale map of the Sea of Japan and indicated point C. "Their orders are to fire on any missile whose trajectory appears to be targeting Japan."

"Even an overshoot?"

"Yes," the colonel said.

Hallam nodded and the Japanese colonel resumed his seat. "Exactly what I would do," he told the Japanese and South Korean liaison colonels. "I admire your governments' willingness to act decisively. Something mine seems reluctant to do."

"So, David," Hallam said to the scholarly looking CIA liaison. "To develop a plan we need to guess Chae's target."

"There are no clear indicators yet," Kyle said calmly. "But we know Chae would like nothing better than to add South Korea's advanced manufacturing facilities to his inventory. North Korea's big, but antiquated land forces might be able to capture the Seoul-Inchon corridor, an area South Korea will not want to fire on."

An army liaison Colonel shook his head, "North Korea's ten thousand tanks have fuel and ammunition for only about a week of full-up engagement..."

"A week is all it would take," Kyle snapped back. The army officer didn't reply.

Hallam turned to his chief of staff. "What's the status of my request to CINCPACFLT for authority to act?"

"Denied. Orders are to assume alert posture, but do not reposition any assets in a way that might be considered provocative."

Hallam snorted as he scanned the grim faces around the table. "Any 'non-provocative' suggestions, gentlemen?"

"This may be a dumb question," a young commander asked, "but do we know this missile will be nuclear armed?"

A red faced Marine Brigadier General huffed, "Yesterday we were told their single operational nuclear warhead was taken from its secure storage site." He leveled a withering glare on the young Navy man. "I'm sure you remember the briefing."

Rogue Patriot

"Are we sure the warhead was moved to the ballistic missile launch site?" Hallam asked mildly. "Or was it moved somewhere else?"

People looked around at each other and finally all eyes came to rest on the hapless Richardson who had moved from parade rest to attention and stared into the middle distance. "Sir, 354th intelligence group cannot confirm exactly where the warhead is. It is not in the manufacture facility."

"You've lost track of their nuclear warhead?" the Marine Brigadier General exploded.

"We know it left the manufacturing facility. We do not know where it is now."

"I'll give you pretty good goddam odds it's at that launch site there!" The Marine stabbed a finger at the screen.

A staff commander came in, sweating profusely, and said to Hallam, "Secretary of Defense needs to speak to you now, sir."

Hallam nodded. "While I'm gone, develop three options for us that are 'non-provocative' and still have a chance to stop this launch."

JD stood also, "I'll excuse myself now, sir. I need to check on whether my people have left for home yet."

"You've completed training our people to operate

9

your drone aircraft, haven't you?" the Navy Vice Admiral asked JD Iselin.

"Yes sir, the SEAL team is fully capable and we've transferred a Ghost II drone to them."

CHAPTER 2

JD walked the four blocks to the training field where his people had been training the SEAL team in use of Ghost II drones. The afternoon heat and humidity were beginning to soften toward evening.

His lead trainer, Fredric 'Flash' Gordon, was under the netting, packing what looked like a grey plastic, four-prop helicopter, about 18" square, into its case. No one else was around.

"Hello, Flash." JD let himself in through the gate. "Ready to go home?"

Flash got to his feet and adjusted the cowboy hat he was never without. "Yeah. But it has been fun training the SEAL team. Those guys are sharp. They'll have no trouble using these things." He wiped sweat off his brow and resettled his hat. "Your big emergency meeting already finished? Got the world's problems solved?"

"Just a short break. I'll need to go back in a few minutes," JD said. He picked up a Ghost II drone. "Don't go to the airport yet. And don't ship this drone out yet either."

"Does that mean I might get some field work?" His tone was hopeful.

"These things tested out OK, didn't they?" JD changed the subject and handed Flash the drone.

"Perfectly. Easy to fly, almost silent, will carry a half-kilo explosive which is enough to disable most weapon electronics with an electromotive pulse. Only drawback is that they only have about a 100-meter control range. Our SEALS are going to have to be at the site where they want to do the damage. Can't sit safe and sound in Japan and blow up stuff in North Korea. By the way, why did we keep that one Ghost boxed up?" He jerked a thumb in the direction of the secure-storage shipping container chained to the wall of the training building.

"That's an experimental model," JD said. "Carries a bigger explosive charge so that the EMP can be conducted at a greater distance, or it can be used like a steerable grenade to put an explosive on

Rogue Patriot

top of enemy troops hiding behind a barrier."

Flash nodded.

"Everything is classified, but if I read Admiral Hallam correctly, you might get your wish yet," JD told Flash. "I'll Call Lori back at the office and tell her to change your ticket to an open departure date."

Flash grinned. "If the operation calls for Ghosts I can still fly them better than the SEALS. They can go as my support." Flash laughed. "They'd hate that, having to support a contractor in an Op."

JD punched a contact on his phone. But it wasn't Lori Turner, his Chief Operating Officer who answered. It was Cheryl, his soon-to-be ex-wife.

JD said nothing, started to disconnect, then said, "Hello Cheryl," slowly.

"JD."

Flash discreetly stepped away, eyebrows raised.

"Sorry, Cheryl, I hit the wrong button on my phone," JD said.

After a silence, "That pretty well says where things are between us, wouldn't you say?"

An image of Cheryl flooded into JD's mind. She was beautiful, with dark hair, deep blue-grey eyes, and the figure of a woman half her age. She was smart, degree from Radcliffe, the only daughter of one of the best known international law attorneys in Washington, in the midst of a substantial career of her own at the State Department. *Why I am divorcing her?* JD wondered. Then he remembered how strained their time together had become.

"Look, JD," Cheryl said, "I make it a point to always take your call no matter how busy I am, but I'm right in the middle of a meeting, and if you just rang me because you hit the wrong button on your phone, I'm hanging up."

"I am really sorry, Cheryl," JD stuttered. "I don't want to...I mean I do want to...talk to you. Not here, not now, not over the phone. But I'll be back in Washington in a few days and I would like for us to have dinner together, to talk about where we're going. OK?"

There was a pause. "Alright, call me when you're back in town and we'll get together for dinner." She disconnected and JD stood there looking at the phone but not seeing it, thinking about how good things had been right after they married six years ago, and how things seemed to have gotten lost in the last couple of years. Now they lived separate lives, both working sixty-hour weeks.

Rogue Patriot

Flash strolled back over to JD and pushed his cowboy hat back on his head. "None of my business, but if I were you and had a chance at a woman like Cheryl, I wouldn't let anything stand in my way." He pushed his hat down low to hide his eyes. JD nodded, phoned Lori and asked her to change the tickets.

"JD, we've got a problem with the Ghost III prototype, the one you've got..." Lori told him.

"Here comes trouble," Flash whispered to JD. He nodded in the direction of a Navy Lieutenant Commander coming through the gate into the training area.

"I'll call you back, Lori. Promise. Just as soon as my conference with Admiral Hallam is over." JD ended the call.

"Smarmy clods like this guy are the reason I left active duty," Flash whispered. "Name's Gary Hare. Comes for a visit every day to see what we are doing out here with our 'toy airplanes'. "

"Hello, guys!" Hare called heartily as he approached. "Training all finished up?"

He held out his hand to JD, who reluctantly shook it. "I'm Gary Hare, base operations."

"JD Iselin, ISO."

Hare grinned a wide grin that made him look both

ingratiating and stupid. "You mercenaries live the easy life." He hooked a thumb at the SEAL barracks. "Those guys have to work for a living."

Flash closed the shipping box and took it to the steel security container and locked it.

JD said nothing.

"But I guess your little toys here ought to make life easier for my SEALS"

His SEALS?

"How far can these little guys fly anyway?"

JD checked his watch. "That's classified. Sorry."

Hare held up his hands. "Just making conversation. Not trying to get state secrets out of you." He laughed a shrill laugh. "Come by the O-club tonight and I'll buy you a beer. You can meet some of the local girls. If secrets are going to be gotten, they are the ones to do it. Japanese girls are beautiful."

JD's phone beeped. "I've got to get back to my meeting."

CHAPTER 3

At the secure communications center, Hallam seated himself at the desk inside the Lexan cube. An aide was already seated there. On the widescreen TV was the Secretary of Defense, flanked by the Chairman of the Joint Chiefs of Staff and the Director of the CIA. "The North Korean missile is still estimated to be launch capable in fourteen hours?" the Secretary of Defense asked.

"We estimate no longer than ten hours from now," Hallam said calmly.

"Activate OpPlan C immediately," the Secretary of Defense told Admiral Hallam.

"Yes sir," Hallam said, nodding to his aide, who communicated the order down the chain of command. Ships, aircraft and Marines were alerted, but OpPlan C was strictly a defense of Japan and stand-by to support South Korea. No ships or planes would alter their normal patrols.

"Sir," Hallam said equably, "request latitude in rules of engagement. Request authority to fire on my order."

The Secretary of Defense shook his head. "Sorry, the answer is no. You do not have authority to fire. Only I will give you that authority, is that clear?" The CIA director reviewed the situation, but none of it was new.

The Secretary of Defense rose from his chair and the screen went dark.

Hallam left the communications facility but instead of going back upstairs to the Operations Center, walked around the Headquarters building to the front entrance and went up to his office. The three Japanese secretary-translators stood as he entered.

"I don't want to be disturbed for a few moments, Mrs. Suzuki. Thank you."

He closed the door, sat down at his desk, and glanced at the daily situation report. Item three noted that ISO had completed the drone training for his SEAL team. Admiral Hallam set the report aside and leaned back in his chair, looking at the large paper map mounted on the wall. It was an old map, depicting Korea as a single nation.

He opened his desk drawer and took out a small hand written note dated yesterday evening, 1800 hours.

> *Bill, I need to see you ASAP.*
> *Captain Henry Adams, MD*
> *Chief Medical Officer*

He folded the note and put it in his pocket, then went to the display case and took out a framed photograph of him, his wife Mary, and their daughter Monica taken more than thirty years ago. Mary had been dead now for almost ten years. Monica had her own life and it did not include him.

At his secure computer he called up a series of classified Operation Plans, selected one and issued an order putting it into effect immediately. Then he put his hat on and left the office, telling Mrs. Suzuki he would be off base for about an hour, then would return to the Operations Center.

CHAPTER 4

Outside the Administration building, the Japanese sky was blue, the immaculately trimmed lawn a deep green, the humid air blowing in from Tokyo Bay seemed almost alive. Hallam found himself smiling as he got in his staff car and told the driver to take him to Motomachi Street.

"Nothing settles the mind so much as the knowledge that one is to be executed in the morning," Hallam quoted silently. He almost laughed out loud. Now that he had received his death sentence, the uncertainty was past. A weight of anxiety lifted from his shoulders.

Hallam had his driver let him off halfway down the eight blocks that comprised Motomachi Street. A street filled with small art galleries, boutique clothing stores, shops filled with gleaming European-made kitchenware. "Wait for me here."

The crowd flowed past him, ordinary Japanese people going about their business. *What if the North Koreans successfully launched a high ballistic shot at Japan, detonated a dirty nuclear fireball over Tokyo, letting a poisonous cloud of radioactive fallout drift south over Yokohama, bringing slow death to all these people?*

Hallam glanced at his watch. *The North Koreans were preparing a launch right now. Their nuclear warhead was unaccounted for, most likely being installed on the Tae Po Dong, the target of the attack unknown. And my own government says to do nothing but sit and wait.*

A sign at a narrow alley advertised Atelier K, Contemporary Art, one flight up. Hallam went in the door and up the narrow flight of stairs.

The woman seated behind a tiny desk near the door stood and bowed. *"Irasshaimase,"* she greeted him in Japanese, then in English, "Welcome."

Hallam nodded, and slowly made his way around the four walls, looking at each painting for a moment before moving on. The woman went down the stairs, then returned a moment later.

The gallery was a single room, twelve by ten meters, hardwood floor, track lights for the art on four walls, a single bench in the middle made of pale Japanese cryptomeria wood.

He was American military so she was undecided as to whether to bring tea, which she always did for Japanese visitors. He moved around the room, thoughtfully examining each painting, then sat on the bench, facing Tomoko's two darkest paintings. She saw that he sat without fidgeting, with his back straight, so she decided to serve tea as she would a Japanese customer.

She brought it to him with strainer and handleless Japanese cup. "*Sumimasen, dozo,*" she said, setting it on the tray on the bench beside him.

"*Domo,*" he replied.

Hallam let his mind unfocus as he stared at the two paintings, one a foggy coastline seen from across a small bay. What appeared to be the exposed rock of a quarry in a small valley. The other painting was a cold bare classroom, eight children in blue uniforms, a teacher, his expression concerned, looking at them from his place at the blackboard. Both paintings were nicely executed but very dark, fearful in tone.

Rogue Patriot

His mind drifted to Dr. Adams' note. Last week's tests had confirmed that his cancer was advanced. At that examination, Dr. Adams had recommended his immediate transfer back to Washington. Hallam had told him he would consider it. In the meantime, no one was to be told of his illness.

Hallam emptied his mind, focusing on only this moment, on breathing in and breathing out.

Hallam drank his tea. "I believe the painter of these paintings is employed at the U.S. Navy base. A Miss Tomoko Hayakawa?"

"Yes," the woman said. She handed Admiral Hallam a short biography printed in Japanese and English. He read it. The artist was Tomoko Hayakawa from his office. Despite her Japanese features, there was something about her that reminded him of his daughter Monica, also an artist.

Hallam approached the woman, "I'd like to buy these two paintings of Miss Tomoko's," he told her. The woman bowed her thanks.

"Will it be possible to take them now?"

"Yes." She took the two paintings down and began wrapping them carefully on the worktable at the back of the gallery.

The photo on the biography captured the same

sadness Hallam had noticed in Miss Tomoko's eyes at the office. Unlike most formal Japanese photos she was looking slightly away from the camera, eyes cast down. He had seen that expression often in his own daughter, Monica.

He could admit it now, his wife Mary had been right after all. He should have chosen a less ambitious career path and spent time with Mary and Monica. He could have changed his career plan, settled for lower rank, and become a satisfied man. The time to make that change had been more than twenty years ago. But he had wanted something more.

Hallam had been at the Naval Postgraduate School in Monterey, getting his master's degree in Asian geopolitics. He had declined campus housing and rented half of a small duplex in Pacific Grove for himself, Mary, and ten-year-old Monica. Every Saturday morning he and Monica would take a long walk together, down the clean silent streets wreathed in morning fog to Lover's Point Park, sometimes stopping for a croissant and hot chocolate at the bakery on Forest Ave. Then they would walk the trail along the coast as the sun began to burn the fog away, past the research station, past the Aquarium, and down Cannery Row stopping in this shop and that as their fancy dictated. Then down Alvarado Street in Monterey to meet Mary for lunch under the cypress trees on the patio at Cafe des Ami.

After lunch they'd walk home, and he would study until dinnertime when they would drive to Carmel to try a new restaurant, a new wine. It had been a magical year.

His mind travelled that familiar path of memory, guided by nostalgia and regret. The smell of Monterey Bay, the crowds on Fisherman's wharf, the quiet of eucalyptus tree shaded streets and the brightly painted Victorian cottages of Pacific Grove. That year in Monterey had been a good one. They hadn't realized it at the time, but it had been the best year of their lives.

Twenty years later cancer claimed Mary. His career had been stellar. He was already being groomed for politics after the Navy. But when Mary died, he turned his back on that, turned down an assignment at the Pentagon and took his current position in Japan. His career suddenly didn't seem to matter any more. He'd spent four years in Japan, career suicide at his rank, being away from Washington DC that long. Monica was now living in Santa Cruz, working in an art gallery, working at her painting.

When he put Tomoko's artist biography in his pocket his fingers touched the note from Adams. Too late for almost everything now. But not too late to make a small gesture of thanks to a young woman on his staff who reminded him of Monica and the life he could have had. The proprietor handed Hallam the carefully wrapped package and he paid her sixty thousand yen, $600, and made his way down the narrow stair and out onto Motomachi street where he gave the two paintings to his driver.

"I'm going to walk to Yamashita Park. Pick me up there in twenty minutes." He made his way down Motomachi Street, then crossed under the freeway bridge into the end of Yamashita Park. At the rose garden he stopped to admire the pale yellow blooms, then continued to the waterfront and stood looking out over Yokohama Bay.

David Kyle quietly joined him. "Counterintelligence is certain you've got a leak in your HQ. CID is working the issue now. The North Koreans operating in Japan use some pretty sophisticated pattern analysis software on U.S. military activities and on Japanese military. It's surprising what can be deduced by just monitoring things like, say, fuel usage—the different kinds of aircraft fuel, jet, helicopter, fixed wing—that are supplied to the base. Compare it month to month. They know our equipment inventory, and the performance characteristics of each piece of equipment. They know our pattern of readiness and training exercises..."

"You're saying that, based on the data you describe, the North Koreans can predict what kind of Operation we will be conducting before we start?"

"In many cases, yes. You can't disguise a destroyer leaving the base, or a Chinook helicopter taking off. They have spotters living all around all the bases."

"So how do you know there's a leak? What you've told me is that they have done only passive analysis, not active spying."

"Until now. But just today one of the secretary-translators in your office, a Miss Shizue Ito, left the office, met with Commander Hare for a quote drink unquote, then left the base.

"Hare is taking the equipment readiness and utilization spreadsheet to his quarters on a laptop, along with fuel requisitions and resupply requirements. A similar report which he has access to, shows ships and aircraft in use, so he knew a mini-submersible was refueled off the coast of North Korea, he knew two SEALS boarded a tiltwing with a Ghost drone and HALO jump gear. Analysts can figure out approximately where our SEALS will go based on that info. They'll notify North Korea's coastal watch system and be looking for parachutes." Kyle studied Hallam's features as he continued. "And perhaps worst of all, Miss Ito will know there have been no orders from CINCPACFLT and that no coordination with South Korean and Japanese forces has taken place. That will indicate to them this is a clandestine operation, and clearly not a training exercise of some sort. CID is monitoring Hare, but they have lost Miss Ito. She will likely deliver her information and leave Yokohama forever. This is that hot."

Hallam watched three seagulls sunning themselves on the seawall. "I wish I had been told Miss Ito and Miss Hayakawa were returned abductees. I would not have assigned them to my office."

"The Japanese Self Defense forces screen them, but they let us assign them where we want. I believe they were on staff before you were assigned here. North Koreans have turned Miss Ito, she's working for them. But there's no evidence Miss Hayakawa is. In any case, the most damaging part of the leak is Commander Hare. He is providing, probably unintentionally, information on our operations to Miss Ito."

Rogue Patriot

Hallam nodded. "I'll have CID move in on Hare." He paused. "I've never understood why North Korea abducts Japanese occasionally, holds them for a few years, then returns them. Been going on for years. Japanese government seems unable to stop it."

"Most obvious explanation is to train the Japanese as moles to work with North Korean intelligence people once they are returned to Japan." Kyle frowned at Landmark Tower, Yokohama's tallest building, white in the midday sun.

"Want to abort the Op?" Kyle asked quietly.

Hallam studied Kyle's unlined face. "No. We need to sabotage that missile launch. But I will see that word gets to the two SEALS, that there may be North Korean militia looking for them. Let's get back to base and start working this." Hallam straightened. "Thanks, David," Hallam said. "I hate to hear this kind of news, that one of our own people is leaking information."

"He's just dumb, not devious," Kyle said.

"That may be worse. Frankly, Mr. Hare is not one of the brightest bulbs in the box. I should have reassigned him a year ago."

Kyle nodded.

The two men walked away in different directions.

At the street, Admiral Hallam got in his waiting staff car and return to his office.

CHAPTER 5

"**A**ppreciate you coming over to Japan to personally train my SEALs with your Ghost system. I understand it went well?" Hallam asked JD.

"Very well. Your SEALS under Rick Callahan are sharp people. They can operate the drones just as well as my people." A little puzzled at why he had been called out of the Ops Center, JD settled himself into a comfortable chair in Hallam's spartan office.

There were no papers on Admiral Hallam's desk. Along one wall was a large display case filled with plaques, citations, and photos. On another wall hung a large paper map of Korea and several pieces of original art.

"You're confident the EMP package fitted on your Ghosts can scramble the guidance system of a missile like the Tae Po Dong 2 we were just looking at in the Ops Center?"

"Yes, I am. A simple, unhardened, guidance system like the ones the North Koreans buy for their missiles is precisely what my Ghosts' EMP charge is designed for."

"Well, that's good, because I have just ordered a four-man SEAL team to go into North Korea and disable the guidance system on the Tae Po Dong 2 we see on the launch platform."

JD was speechless.

Hallam nodded, "Nobody knows this yet except the SEAL team, and the aircraft and ship COs who'll get them into North Korea. Not CINCPACFLT, not the JCS, not the President of the United States."

"Authorization?" JD said quietly.

Hallam smiled. "The best kind. My conscience."

"Repercussions could be intense."

"The results of a nuclear missile strike could also be intense," Hallam countered.

Iselin thought for a moment. Hallam seemed calm, fully cognizant of what he was doing, and confident it was the right thing.

"We've known each other for twenty five years," JD said. "This action is, shall I say, a little unexpected."

Rogue Patriot

"But logical and timely," Hallam told him.

"It will cost your career,"

Hallam said nothing.

"If you'd told me this is what you had in mind, I would have kept my team here. If ISO did the Op it would maintain the Navy's plausible deniability. If things went bad you could have blamed ISO."

Hallam grinned. "I appreciate the offer, I truly do, but I don't want to hide behind plausible deniability. Your team is gone. Callahan and his men will handle this. If they get in and out undetected, as planned, the missile will simply veer off-course and no one will guess why."

"Sabotaging a missile launch will only slow down North Korean aggressiveness; it won't stop it," JD said.

"True. But it buys time for us, all of us. Time for the U.S. to build detente with the Chinese. They have even more to lose from an unstable North Korea than we do. And a full-up war on the Korean peninsula helps no one."

Hallam sat quietly. JD wondered if he was waiting for further comment. He said, "If I were in your place, I'd do what you've done. I mean that. Hesitation, followed by knee-jerk, poorly thought out interventions, has been the American military response for a generation. It's time to change that. This Op is well thought out, and despite the high stakes, it's low risk."

Hallam rose and shook JD's hand. "Thanks. I trust my people implicitly, but I also need you, who I've considered a friend for my whole career, to tell me if this is wise or not. And you need not be concerned about my career. It's over in any case."

"It is wise." JD grinned. "What if I'd said it was the dumbest thing I'd ever heard of?"

Hallam smiled, something JD had not seen in the two weeks he'd been in Japan. "I would have thanked you for your opinion and proceeded anyway."

As JD got to the practice field he heard a tiltwing roar off the airfield. Callahan and his team would be on North Korean soil within two hours. If this mission was not successful, the international consequences could be dire. He and Hallam had skirted that issue. If the North Koreans actually fired a nuclear weapon on some nation, any nation, it could easily trigger a war.

He put that out of his mind and pressed the lock combination to let himself into the screened practice field. Fredric "Flash" Gordon, was packing equipment into carry-boxes with the ISO emblem on them. A

Rogue Patriot

shipping container stood open in the shade of one wall of the close-combat practice house.

"Must be a hot one," Flash said nodding toward where the tiltwing was disappearing into the western sky. "SEALS bolted out of here like blue lightning."

"How many?"

"Callahan plus one."

"You checked the EMP charges on their Ghost II, right?" JD asked Flash.

Flash nodded, "Checked and rechecked."

"What about this Ghost III here?" Flash hooked a thumb at a sealed carry-case in the steel freight container. "I'm thinking that's what I'm going to be using in our part of this operation." His tone was hopeful.

"No, sorry. We've got no part in this operation."

Flash ducked his head, lips curled.

"I know, training is not as sexy as doing," JD told him. "But you're good at it. In any case you're to stay in full readiness for the next eight hours. Get your gear, full set, and get over to the airfield. There's another tiltwing there. If Callahan's team succeeds, you won't be needed. If something goes wrong, I'm betting Admiral Hallam will want you and me to go in and save their bacon. But leave that Ghost in its box if we're called on to go help them out, the opportunity for EMPing the missile will already have passed."

"So we're the back-up team? Flash made it sound like a disease.

"Yes, the back-up team, JD told him. "But on the bright side, as of right now, you're on full combat pay."

"The Op what I think it is?" Flash drawled. Even though he had been born and raised in Southern California, he favored western shirts, cowboy hats, and a Texas drawl. "Go burn that North Korean missile's guidance?"

JD nodded. "Yeah."

Flash laughed out loud. "But the news says the U.S. official posture is not to make any provocative moves, but stay ready..." he took his cowboy hat off, wiped his brow, and put it back on. "While we're standing around being 'ready' they're launching. I guess that's why Admiral Hallam decided the best defense is a good offense."

JD grinned. "No comment."

Flash finished packing the training equipment. "I'll get my gear and get to the airfield."

"One more thing," JD said. "If we get the signal to go in, it's going to be hot. The mission will have been

Rogue Patriot

compromised and it won't be good. I'll tell you the same thing I've told you before every Op I've ever asked you to undertake: if you don't want to go, you don't have to. No questions asked. You'll still retain combat pay for the duration of this one. I'll rotate you to the next Op."

Flash grinned, "And miss all the fun? Not me. I'm rarin' to go. Besides, I'm the only one you've got, you sent the rest of our team home yesterday."

CHAPTER 6

The coffee shop at Sogo department store was busy. Tomoko and Shizue sat in the waiting area for twenty minutes before they were given a table. But the table was nice, as it overlooked the atrium of the big department store crowded with smartly dressed women shoppers.

As they studied their menus, printed in elegant English and Japanese, Shizue asked, "Has Tanaka-san sold any of your paintings at Atelier K?"

"Let's don't talk about them," Tomoko said.

"Why not?" Shizue said. "I know they are of the school in North Korea. You painted them to make your nightmares go away."

"Don't you have nightmares from those days?" Tomoko said truculently.

"No."

Tomoko told her, "Talk about something else."

"Let's talk about clothes. You should buy new clothes."

"I don't have enough money," Tomoko glanced around at the crowded department store coffee shop, the women impeccably dressed. "I can't buy new shoes every week like you do."

Shizue studied Tomoko from behind a haze of cigarette smoke. "Maybe you should make more money, then you can buy what you want."

"Talk about something else."

Shizue turned her mouth down. "You are not very happy this afternoon, telling me not to talk about this, about that."

"Sorry, I was in the office all day Saturday, and didn't sleep well last night..."

"Hare-kun was up late last night too," Shizue said. "Unusual."

"Why do you see him? You tell me he is boring and he talks all the time about boring things. And all in English, not even two words of Japanese. Water lines and traffic and fuel and what ships are where."

Shizue lit a Marlboro. "Boring, boring, but they pay me for it."

Tomoko frowned into her teacup. "That is wrong."

Shizue laughed a small sarcastic laugh, "Hare-kun endlessly talking, scattering his reports around his room. I copy things from his laptop he leaves lying around while he is at Officers club drinking. He talks all the time but says nothing." She made a gesture signifying baby talk and both women laughed. "Last night he goes out at 11 PM. Usually by then he's drunk, but last night was different. He only drank three beers. I wait for him because I think he will come back soon, but he doesn't, so I leave at midnight. Usually I leave at 11..."

"After..." Tomoko hinted.

Shizue ignored the innuendo. "This afternoon he comes back to change uniform. I was there copying his files. He noticed nothing. Only thinks of himself. He tells me he thinks a tiltwing has flown to North Korea with two—'animal men'—I can't think of the English word."

Shizue paused while the waiter came with another pot of tea. She seemed to be studying him. After he'd gone Tomoko said, "You were staring at him." Shizue laughed and poured tea for both of them.

Shizue stubbed out her cigarette, checked the time, and stood up. "I have to catch my train." Shizue touched the slim white envelope lying on the white tablecloth. An envelope like all the others Tomoko had watched Shizue exchange for money here at the coffee shop. "This is important information, but I am going away. I paid back the Yakuza but still they threaten. I am supposed to get more information. But I won't do it any more. When the waiter takes this envelope and leaves an envelope with money, you keep the money. Spend it on new clothes."

Tomoko was speechless, "You're going away? For how long?"

For once Shizue's confidence was not there, her voice seemed different. "I don't know. A long time. I've worked here for two years, that's long enough. I think maybe I will go to Osaka." She gathered her purse and stood to go.

Tomoko stood up too. "I don't want you to go."

Shizue bowed slightly. "Thank you, Tomoko-chan. You have been a good friend, my best friend, but I have to leave. Pass this information, keep the money, and tell people you don't know where I went. I think they will ask about me. They seem suspicious."

"What about Hare-san?"

"Tell him nothing."

She made her way between the crowded tables and out the door.

Tomoko touched her teacup, but did not drink any more. She felt abandoned again, even though Shizue was a not a good friend. She was as self-centered as the Americans.

The coffee shop was very crowded; the waiter was busy. The slim envelope still lay on the white tablecloth. Tomoko opened it, inside was a flash drive and a one-page summary. She copied the Japanese summary into her notebook and put it in her purse.

She started to leave with the envelope, but realized, *if I don't make this exchange, Shizue may get into more trouble. Yakuza could find her. I will exchange this envelope, then tell Mrs. Suzuki about it at the office and give her the money and this copy.*

About fifteen minutes later, the waiter cleared the teacups and the white envelopes were exchanged.

In the concourse under the department store that led to the train station, Tomoko opened the envelope and counted the money. One hundred thousand yen—about a thousand U.S. dollars. She put it with her copy of the summary Shizue had written.

CHAPTER 7

JD was admitted to the Ops Center and took his customary seat. Hallam was not there. "Progress?" he asked the Chief of Intel.

"The aircraft with the SEAL team is at the drop zone," The petty officer operating the big screen told the men in the room. He designated a point on the detailed map of the launch site. A picture-in-picture appeared with a close-up of the missile from a Global Hawk. JD could see the missile stacked on the pad, fuel lines connected. A North Korean crew was monitoring the fueling.

He checked his watch even though there was a row of digital clocks above the screen. One displayed North Korean local time. The chronometer on screen said local sunup at the missile sight would be within fifty minutes.

The intelligence chief split the screen to show the ravine where the two SEALS were expected to touch down.

At twenty thousand feet the titlwing slowed. A flat electronic screen, its display in red to preserve night vision, showed the aircraft track, the two SEALs' exit point, the coastline, the landing point, and the missile site one kilometer inland.

The crew chief came back and got a thumbs-up from both SEALS. He activated the ramp, which slowly declined, while Rick and Seth checked each other's back, then knelt on the aluminum deck. The red light over the ramp came on.

The air was cold. Outside, under a high overcast, the night was entirely dark. Callahan felt the endorphins rise in his blood. In a few second they'd be out in the night sky, and a minute after that, on the ground in enemy territory. He glanced at Seth hugging his SM-24 combination sniper and assault weapon. Seth grinned back. This was what being a SEAL was all about.

The ramp stabilized at horizontal, the screen showed the aircraft at the exit point, and the light over the ramp turned green. The two SEALS got to their feet and charged off the back of the ramp into thin air.

A few seconds of silence as his velocity increased, then the familiar roar of air as Rick fell, in stable position watching the screen on the top of his belly pack, which showed the landing zone's location and his altitude.

They'd open low, five hundred feet above the ground. Surface winds were forecast to be calm. Rick tilted his arms to steer his body on the air rushing past, keeping the red dot that was him centered on the bulls eye of the canopy deploy point. At altitude he pulled the ripcord, the chute billowed smoothly out and he was hanging in silence over the dark North Korean countryside. Seth's chute was fifty meters away. They steered down into the ravine and touched down lightly in scraggly bushes.

In a moment they had slid free and rolled the filmy black synthetic material of their chutes into small bundles tucked under a bush. They stayed down for a moment listening, but there were no sounds except crickets. The smell was of dusty leaves, rocky soil, and a hint of the ocean just three kilometers to the east.

Seth indicated he would go up to the ridgetop as they had planned and do a careful 360-degree scan of the area with his night vision goggles. He made his way through waist-high scrub brush toward the ridgetop. Rick memorized the route he was taking, then unpacked the Ghost drone and ran a quick check of it and the controller.

Both were fully functional. He stowed the drone and went to join Seth lying under the scrubby brush on the ridgeline. Seth gave him the thumbs up—no sign of human activity. Rick switched on the controller uplink, got the steady green light, and held a signal button down for three seconds. The signal would go up to a satellite and be relayed back to the Yokosuka Operations Center indicating they had landed safely and were making their way toward the missile site.

A steady red light stayed on after Callahan had ended his signal. This was supposed to indicate an incoming coded message, but the little square screen didn't light with text. *Could be we're not in a clear position,* Rick thought.

He switched it off so he and Seth could move through the darkness to the missile sight. He'd check it again when they were in position on the hill above the missile site.

In twenty minutes they were overlooking the

short valley where the missile launch site had been constructed.

The railroad spur that came from the main line following the coast ended at rolling doors covering the face of a cave on the south side of the valley. The launch platform was built into the north side of the valley.

The 150-ton mobile crane that had been used to stack the missile's three stages was parked almost straight below him at the head of the semicircular valley.

Several work lights illuminated the four metal catwalks that ringed the rocket. A crew was standing by at the fueling hoses that snaked off to the propellant storage tanks. A gas-powered Honda generator on a pickup truck purred, powering the work lights and the fuel pumps.

It would be light in two hours. If all went well, they would have disabled the missile guidance, made their way back to the cove on the coast, and been picked up by a sea skimmer. They'd be in the mini-submersible, and underwater before dawn.

Rick scanned the area with his night vision scope while Seth set up his weapon, snapped up the scope, and began a thorough scan of the area below them.

"Two guard teams, each with one dog," Seth told Rick over the hard wire intercom. "Alternating pattern, ten minute sweeps past the gantry tower steps."

"Understood." Rick told him. "I want to fly the ghost down the missile in between the guard's sweeps close to it. They won't be looking up, but that fueling crew might, so I need to wait a minute and see if they will move away from the missile."

"Don't wait too long," Seth reminded him. "Briefing said they'd probably launch within thirty minutes of completing fueling."

"Understood. But that's good, the warhead and guidance will already be in place, so it will only take me a couple of minutes to EMP it."

Rick quickly unpacked the Ghost and the controller package. The little grey drone looked incongruously like a toy sitting at Rick's feet. "If I can make the recon with this drone before they know..."

Below, the fueling crew stood around waiting for the pumps to fill the tanks as the guards continued their circuits.

The text screen came on again on Callahan's belly pack when he activated the drone's uplink. Callahan

Rogue Patriot

pressed and held the receive button but a nonsense string of letters scrolled across the tiny screen.

"Operations is trying to tell us something," Rick told Seth, "Signal is not coming through. Hope our uplink works better than the downlink."

Callahan activated and calibrated the drone as he'd been taught, then, using the joysticks, lifted off the ground silently.

"Guards are at their farthest," Seth told Rick. "Also, looks like the fueling crew is about finished. Two men have gone down to the tanks, there's one man left on the gantry and he's occupied with the hose fittings."

Callahan flew the drone up off the ground and let its autonomous guidance take it across a hundred feet of air to the warhead fairing on the rocket. Fortunately none of the work lights were pointing up. The drone went directly to the correct point on the missile, where the main engine guidance system was located. It slowly circled the missile.

On Rick's laptop, the view from the drone showed the smooth skin of the missile. Two sets of sensors were activated, one for the guidance electronics, batteries, and capacitors, and the other for the warhead plutonium and uranium 235.

"Got the electronics," Rick whispered into his throat

microphone. He watched the four lines of readouts vary as the drone came slowly around the missile.

"No radioactives though." The drone was half way around. In a minute it had completed a full circuit and hovered silently at the side of the missile away from the North Koreans below.

No radioactives. Rick stared at the display. "Maybe they don't have the warhead mounted yet. Which means I'm going to have to run the Ghost into their shop area."

"Guards maintaining their circuit," Seth whispered. "And nothing behind us." Rick kept the drone hovering, but on the opposite side from the team of guards passing below. He confirmed that the readings had been recorded for later uplink, then darkened his screen and checked the time. They needed to start for the coast in five minutes.

Callahan quickly flew the Ghost down to the top of the big rolling doors that covered the face of the cave that had been converted to workshop space.

"The fueling crew has all the hoses off the missile and are stowing them."

Just then a personnel door opened and a Korean in civilian clothes strolled out, yawning. Callahan ducked the Ghost in the door and quickly let it rise up to the cave ceiling on self-guidance. On his screen he could see the layout of the workshop. He just had time for one pass down the length of the workshop.

That sweep told him there were no missile components on any of the worktables and no residual traces of radioactive materials in the shop area. The Ghost rose back up to the ceiling above the big lights and hovered in darkness. He quickly reviewed the recorded data. No radioactives in the warhead or in the shop, but the chemical sniffer readings went off the scale. "Nitrate explosives." Callahan whispered.

"Guards coming," Seth told him.

Callahan moved the Ghost down to the personnel door. The civilian had gone back inside, but the door stood open waiting for the fueling crew to come inside. Callahan took the opportunity to fly the ghost out and quickly straight up into the dark sky.

The fueling crew, noticing nothing, hurried inside and closed the door.

Callahan flew the Ghost back up to the warhead and clicked the sensors over to chemical explosives and confirmed the presence of chemical explosives. Rick triggered the ultrasonic pulses that would record a rough image of what was inside the warhead fairing.

"Time to move out, boss," Seth told him.

"Right," Callahan said. He enabled the Ghost's internal explosive charge, put it up close to the side of the missile where the guidance system was housed and pressed the trigger.

There was a snap like a .22 shot, and the twisted plastic remains of the drone fell into darkness behind the metal gantry.

The red light was still flashing on Rick's downlink screen, but no text message. He stowed the drone controller in his belly pack.

"Time to move out," he told Seth, "I'm disconnecting the intercom. Extinguish all indicator lights and move out."

One of the guard teams stopped their patrolling, started one of the two trucks, and turned its headlights on, then sat idling.

Hopefully just moving the trucks back for the launch, Rick thought as he and Seth scrambled through the brush toward the coast.

Rick and Seth moved quickly through brush and across dry winter rice paddies terraced into the ravine sides.

They were at the bottom of the last ravine before the coast when cross fire from two automatic rifles opened up on them.

CHAPTER 8

Miraculously, no rounds hit either Rick or Seth, but a ricochet sprayed rock chips and Seth went down.

Rick crawled over to him. There was blood on the belly of his camo blouse. He pulled his shirt up and saw there was a profusely bleeding flesh wound just below the ceramic body armor plate.

Rick ripped open two steripads, "This is going to hurt a little," he told Seth and without waiting, wiped the blood away with one pad and pressed the other one on the wound, at the same time feeling for how deep the slash was. "Didn't slice your peritoneum, no protruding guts. It's a flesh wound."

Seth groaned and tried to sit up but Rick pushed him back down.

"We're just below the top of the last ridge," Rick

told him. "Those troops are going to be cautious coming up the slope toward us, we've got time to rest a minute."

"They'll try to go around us," Seth mumbled through a clenched jaw.

"They don't know how many of us there are." Rick hoped that statement was true. "You set up right here. I'm going to look over the ridge. See if our taxi is here yet."

Rick helped Seth set up his weapon. "If anything moves down there, kill it."

Rick eased through the brush to the top of the ridge. As he peered out over the flat ocean he realized dawn was breaking. No North Koreans in sight anywhere up or down the rocky cove, the railroad line or the railroad spur into the missile site.

Rick's screen on his belly-pack came to life, clear text: *NK aware of your presence and in pursuit. Max strength 6 pax.*

"This thing is finally working right," Rick muttered. He hit the acknowledge button. Just then another message appeared, *Sea skimmer delayed, hold position for approx twenty minutes.*

He began making his way back to where Seth was

Rogue Patriot

hiding when he heard Seth's rifle snap off a shot, then another, and another. Rick slid down through the brush to him.

Hallam returned to his seat in the Operations Center and waved the Marine Brigadier General over. "SEAL situation?"

"Not good, sir." He stood straight-backed and respectful, but exuded *I told you so*.

Hallam swiveled in his chair and invited the Marine BG to sit down.

The Marine BG remained standing. He snapped a glance at the row of clocks on the wall all set to different time zones. "It will be dawn soon in North Korea. Our OpPlan called for having the skimmer pick the men up before dawn, get out to the submersible, and get underwater before first light."

"Why are you reminding me of this, John?" Hallam said evenly.

The Navy Captain in charge of sea operations turned on the Marine BG and for a moment it looked like they might come to blows. "We've finally been able to contact the SEALS so they know it's only a platoon searching for them."

Mike Trial

"Only a platoon..." the Marine BG said tightly.

"Sir! We have the upload from the drone," a petty officer interrupted.

"Liquid oxygen is venting from missile ports now, sir," Richardson said. "They are ready to launch."

"Put the drone upload on the screen," Hallam directed, "But split the screen and show me the situation on the ground with the SEALS and enemy troops."

"How did those North Korean troops know to be at that exact spot before dawn?" the Marine BG barked at the Navy Captain.

"Cool off, you two!" Hallam snapped.

Callahan and Seth lay under the scrub brush watching for movement in the ravine when a giant booming crackle came across the still dawn. The rocket engines throttled up with a cough, like the biggest veldt lion ever imagined. The noise escalated to a sustained roar so loud it seemed to ripple the air. The missile lifted off over the ridges and rose on a column of flame and noise.

"Keep your eyes on the ravine," Callahan told Seth. "Those troops may take this opportunity to rush us."

With ponderous grace the white missile rose above them, picking up speed. The noise was bone-shaking as the missile continued rising, arcing gracefully away

Rogue Patriot

to the East. The contrail began to drift and dissipate.

Rick decided to risk opening his tablet computer so he could study the map. There was a text message from the Op Center: *Skimmer will be on the beach in thirty minutes.*

Thirty more minutes, Rick thought with dismay. He checked his ammo. Four magazines left.

"Let's see the upload," Hallam said. The big screen lit with the video Callahan's Ghost had filmed of the Tae Po Dong 2 missile twenty minutes earlier. Richardson put the data up on the screen and told everyone the conclusion—the warhead on the missile was not nuclear.

Hallam thought this over, then turned to his chief of staff. "Get Kyle."

The video the Ghost had taken moved down the side of one missile to the rocket nozzles.

"Russian-made rocket motors," Kyle said, "RD-180's."

The images from the drone moved back up the missile to the warhead. "Here's what's inside," Richardson said, and put what looked like a sonogram on the screen. "Not a nuclear warhead."

David Kyle studied the screen in silence.

"Well?" Hallam asked finally.

"Guidance batteries and capacitances matches the profile, so our EMP probably disabled the main guidance. We'll find out soon enough. But the warhead is conventional explosives plus several hundred two-centimeter diameter steel spheres." He pointed at a series of squiggles on a screen. "A big shotgun shell."

The video from the Ghost's recon of the inside of the shop came up. "No residual radioactives from handling equipment or protective gear. There hasn't been any weapons grade nuclear material in this shop area."

The Ghost came back tracking down the length of the building in the shadows above the lights, then crossed to the missile, located the main guidance access panel and the screen went blank.

There was silence in the Operations Center.

A petty officer broke the silence, "Message from Space Command, sir."

"Put it on the screen," Richardson said.

"That missile is going into an elliptical orbit around the earth and will burn up on reentry over the south Atlantic." There was a global view on the screen with the missile's warhead projected as yellow line wrapping around the planet; a long ellipse, not a ballistic arc. Richardson walked up to the screen as though he could see through it. "I think I know what they were trying to do, and they may still succeed. This wasn't a ballistic launch at all. They intended to put that warhead into the orbit of our communications and intelligence satellites, then fire the shotgun. Those steel balls would blow dozens of satellites out, cripple half the international communications, both military and commercial."

"Space Command advises North Korean missile controllers are using all their third stage fuel to try to correct."

"Will they make it?"

"Looks like they'll have one incoming pass through the satellite belt before the warhead re-enters the atmosphere and incinerates."

"How soon?"

"About ninety minutes from now, sir."

Hallam stood and stared at the yellow arc, "So satellite navigation and communication are going to be at risk in about an hour and half. Our ships, aircraft, troops, are all dependent on satellite-base navigation and communication. Get word to CINCPACFLT and the Secretary of Defense, if Space Command hasn't already done so."

CHAPTER 9

JD stepped outside the building to take a call from his office in the States on his cell phone. "Dammit, your timing is terrible, Lori. I need to be..."

"I just got a call from the bank in Reston," Lori told him. "Harrison called personally, said they were terminating our credit line, which as you know we have been using to fund operating expenses, including Matt's salary. We owe a quarter of a million right now. I can't pay Matt to figure out how to fix Ghost III unless I get some cash right now. Or a promise of revenue I can show the bank. Can you get the Navy to give you a letter of intent to purchase?"

"Lori," JD said, exasperated, "I need a fix for it before I can sell it to the Navy."

Rogue Patriot

JD noticed Lt. Commander Hare coming out of the HQ building. Hare saw JD, quickly turned and hurried off the opposite direction. *What's he doing here at five in the morning? He's a base maintenance guy,* JD wondered.

"I'll try to think of something," JD told Lori, "I'll call you back as soon as I can." He clicked his phone off and went into the HQ building Hare had exited.

Ms. Suzuki was attempting to console Tomoko, who had her face in her hands, crying.

JD tried to put a sympathetic smile on his face. "Is anything wrong?" Tomoko stopped sobbing. Mrs. Suzuki was talking to her very fast in Japanese. For a moment JD stood not knowing what to do. He crossed to the glass cube that was his office. *Can't solve her problems right now, got to solve my own.*

He opened his laptop and scrolled through folders for a few moments. He noticed Tomoko gather up her things and leave the office. Mrs. Suzuki looked vexed, but returned to her own desk and resumed her work. JD sauntered over to her desk. "I appreciate you staying at your desk overnight. I hope Miss Tomoko is alright?" He phrased it as a question but Mrs. Suzuki only bowed and said nothing. JD did not know that Japanese custom dictated that no junior member of an office went home until the most senior person there went home.

"Is there a report for me from Com Center?" JD asked Mrs. Suzuki.

Ms. Suzuki handed him an envelope addressed to him, with security seals. He retreated to his glass walled office, took out the typed pages, and began reading. It was a preliminary report on the Ghost III warhead instability. JD struggled through the chemistry. "Too tightly packed a charge, but since the EMP effect deteriorates by inverse square, we've got to have four times the explosive to double the range." *And that's what's in the Ghost III.* He knew it was an experimental explosive they'd bought from THK last year.

JD slapped the report down on his desk and checked his watch. He'd been gone from Ops for twenty minutes already.

"Operations Center, says you are needed there immediately," Mrs. Suzuki told him. She continued to stand at his desk side.

"Is there something else?" he asked, scowling at his watch. "I have to go to the Ops Center now." She stood rigid, almost shivering. "Is something wrong?" he asked. He noticed a typed message in her left hand. "What is it?"

Rogue Patriot

She stood silent for a few more seconds, then handed him the paper, "Miss Tomoko said to give this to you. She asked you not discuss it with Lt. Commander Hare."

"Was Hare in here a few minutes ago?" Mrs. Suzuki's normally impassive face drained of all color. She remained silent.

"I know he was," JD said. "I saw him come out. If he is the cause of Miss Tomoko's difficulties, I will attend to that later." JD checked his watch again. "Right now I have to return to the Ops Center. If you speak to Miss Tomoko tell her take today off. Tell her to go home."

Mrs. Suzuki nodded.

They both stood there a moment. An idea occurred to JD. "Home equity," he said to an uncomprehending Mrs. Suzuki. He returned to his office, opened his laptop and quickly wrote an email to his bank in Maryland. "A hundred thousand to ISO should tide us over." I'll try to explain this to Cheryl later, he thought, dreading that day.

After he was done, he looked at the typewritten sheet Mrs. Suzuki had said Tomoko had left for him. A frown knotted his forehead. Got to get this info to the Ops Center.

At the Ops Center, Hallam was waiting for JD. He walked him to the small conference table at the back of the Operations center. "We've got a problem and I need your help," Hallam said directly.

"I think I know what it is," JD said handing him the sheet of paper. "Your staff leaked the fact that we've got SEALs on the ground in North Korea."

Hallam nodded. "Our SEALS are already trading shots with the North Koreans, and our pick up skimmer is delayed dodging a North Korean patrol boat."

Hallam studied his hands on the glass top of the table. Behind him the big board showed only the scrubland at the Korean coast, the railroad track along the ocean and the dull grey Pacific.

Hallam looked haggard. "A North Korean platoon from the missile site guard detachment was sent up there based on this intelligence report. They somehow found out about our operation. If the SEALs are captured, it will be a major international incident, I don't need to tell you. But what truly bothers me, JD, is that those two young men will have been sacrificed in my attempt to prevent an escalating military situation, and the reverse will happen. The situation will escalate."

Rogue Patriot

"I have one man still here on base, trained and ready to go," JD said. "That could be the deciding factor for the SEALs in a firefight with a small contingent of enemy troops."

JD stood up. "Where's your man now?"

"At the airfield, equipped and ready to go. And he is current on weapons and HALO."

"Can you direct him to go in alone? I don't need to tell you how high risk this is."

JD straightened up. "He'll go. If he were standing here right now he would already have volunteered."

Hallam stood up and shook JD's hand. "I'll authorize the flight and notify the SEALS and the sea skimmer. Tell your man what we're going to try to do. They can work out the details while he's enroute."

JD nodded, picked up the phone at the end of the glass table, and got Flash on the line and outlined the situation. "But it's up to you. If you don't want..."

"I'm on it. Contact me enroute with latest info." In the background JD could hear the tiltwing's engines starting to spool up.

"One SEAL has an injury, so it's you and Callahan against possibly a whole platoon of North Koreans."

"Boss, I'd call those even odds. Now get off the line and let me get to work."

"Good man!" JD said.

Flash laughed, "I'll be in and out before you know it. My ex-wife always used to criticize me for that." He broke the connection.

That crazy sonofabitch, JD thought. *But if anybody can do this, he can.*

CHAPTER 10

Rick and Seth were at the top of the last ridgeline. They lay under the dark green bushes that grew everywhere in coastal North Korea. Nothing between them and open water but a ragged slope, the railroad tracks that ran along the coast on an embankment, and the black and grey sand of a small cove.

Thank God for that solid gray overcast, Rick thought. Seth's side was swollen but blood flow had stopped. "Rock chips may have cracked a rib," Seth grunted between clenched teeth. "Can't move very fast."

Rick had forced Seth to take some morphine to suppress the pain so he could move fast when the time came, but it made him babble.

"It's already light," Seth chattered on. "We were supposed to be out of here before dawn."

"Yeah. But our ride won't be here for another fifteen minutes."

"If we wait too long they'll have men down on the beach. Cut us off."

"They don't know how many of us are here, and they don't know how we plan to get out, so they're going to be cautious. They probably figure we might send a platoon of our own troops onto the beach to blast them back while we get out and they don't want to risk that, so I guess they've decided to lie low until they can get reinforcements."

Just then he saw movement along the ridgeline inland. "Oh shit!" Rick said. "Here they come." A squad of North Korean troops was coming forward, by ones and twos.

"Good training," Rick said quietly, sighting his weapon. "Staggered advance, random times. Let them get close."

"What the hell would regular army troops be doing out here?" Seth asked not taking his eye off the sight of his weapon.

"Probably guarding the missile site," Rick said. He wished Seth would shut up. "Maybe they found out about us being here. Maybe there was an intelligence leak. Keep your mind on your shooting. As soon as we open fire they'll realize there only two of us and they may try an assault. When they start across that dry rice paddy at the bottom of the ravine, we blast them. Let the first one get almost all the way across."

Seth grunted a chuckle that obviously hurt. "Remember that tee shirt you used to wear, off duty, back in San Diego when we were trainees?"

After a moment a grin broke over Callahan's face. "Yeah, I remember. I guess I was a cocky little bastard back then, wasn't I?"

"Still are. You loved that slogan, *Fear is temporary, regret is forever.*"

"Hold on," Rick pressed his earbuds. "Got an incoming message." He listened for a moment then turned to Seth.

"ISO guy, Flash, has HALO'd in, is coming up behind the Koreans right now, going to open fire on them, confuse them enough that with covering fire from us, he can run straight to us, through the middle. We shoot anyone we see to either side then get down to the beach. Sea skimmer's almost here."

"I can do that," Seth grunted through his pain.

"How much ammo have you got?"

"Three magazines of twenty."

"As soon as Flash opens fire, put your weapon on

auto and fire all your ammo at the troops to your left, I'll do the same to the right. As soon as you are out of ammo get down to the beach as fast as you can. Got it?"

"Got it."

Flash scrambled up the slope and peered into the ravine. He immediately caught sight of the backs of five North Koreans moving stealthily down the slope. The lead man was just about to cross the dry rice paddy at the bottom. It was light but the sky was still a solid grey. He checked his ammo: four full magazines plus one in his weapon.

He clicked on his body camera with audio, went prone, adjusted his sling and sighted on one man, then the second, then back to the first, controlled his breathing, fired once, which dropped the first one, swung to where his eye and mind already had the second one pegged and dropped him, then swung back scanning for more.

There was movement in several places. A fusillade of shots came from the top of the ridge ahead. Flash sprayed a full magazine of suppressing fire in an arc in front of him, reloaded, got to his feet and ran straight down the slope, across the dry paddy, and up to the ridgeline trusting the SEALS would recognize him. Shots spanged up and down the ravine. Flash made it to the top of the ridge in under two minutes and dived into the clump of scrubby brush where Rick and Seth were hiding.

Then the three of them were on their feet, Flash and Rick helping Seth, and they half-slid, half fell, down the slope to the rocky scrabble at the bottom. Seth got to his feet, completely disoriented. Flash and Rick grabbed him and hustled him across the railroad track and down the embankment to the black sand beach.

The sea skimmer, a slab-sided grey shape, about ten meters long, all six fans roaring, raced straight at them on its cushion of air. Its dull grey radar-absorbing paint and sloping flat sides made it look like a stealth fighter without wings. At the beach, it slowed and pivoted, blasting them with sand. The rear hatch opened. A Marine in armor inside the skimmer signaled them to get on board. Rick and Flash threw Seth onto the aluminum door ramp and rolled onto it. The ramp started closing and the skimmer ran for the horizon.

Rick slid over to check Seth, who was now unconscious. "Brace him down!" the Marine roared through the racket. Rick and Flash got him situated, then cinched themselves in.

"Not much like the old M113s is it?" Flash shouted at Callahan, grinning.

Rick tapped the panel behind his head and shouted back, "Damned glad to get behind some steel."

The Marine rapped a knuckle on the panel. "Not steel. Fiber composite. Won't stop a rifle round."

"How fast will this thing go?" Flash asked.

"Sixty knots, on a flat sea."

Flash took his helmet off, pulled a shapeless wad out of his pack, and straightened it into his battered cowboy hat, which he settled on his head.

"Hey, that was fun," he shouted to Rick. "We'll have to do this more often."

CHAPTER 11

Iselin hurried down to the secure communications room and was checked in. On the screen, Lori's narrow face looked very tired.

"The Ghost III explosive charge has a problem," she told JD. "Our team is just back from testing at Yuma Proving Ground. We're going to have to do some redesign..."

"I've only got a few minutes," Iselin said. "What's wrong with it?"

"The explosive, it's unstable. It's a very dense pack according to Matt, so over a short period of time it destabilizes," Lori said looking at a report on another screen. "Could go off without being triggered."

"If the vehicle works, I can still demonstrate it to the Navy even though we can't have a live fire..."

"Where is your Ghost III stored, and is the explosive out of it?"

"In a secure storage container on the training field," JD told her. "But I think Flash left the explosive in."

"Well, don't handle it," Lori said. "The explosive is three months old. Well into the time frame for instability."

"If it goes off in that container, the Navy will just lose one steel container. I'm not planning to take it out..."

"Don't handle it in any way," Lori's tone was sharp. "Get the Navy's ordnance explosives team to dispose of it."

"I hear you," JD told her. He checked his watch. "I need to go. Tell Matt to work on a fix. I want an update in 24 hours. And if he can buy some redesigned explosive you can ship it to me and I can still demonstrate Ghost III to the Navy while I'm here."

In the Operations Center JD took a seat beside Kyle who was sitting silently reading his laptop. "Status of the SEAL team?" JD asked.

"One SEAL sustained a flesh wound, your guy is fine. Submersible should have them back here in about six hours."

Richardson came over to Kyle. "Sir, here's something puzzling. May have nothing to do with this missile launch, but...look at this." He signaled to a subordinate who put some fuzzy three-meter resolution images up on the screen.

"Early this morning, before dawn, two North Korean fishing trawlers, spy boats, came in close to shore at an unpopulated part of the Chinese coast, north of the city of Lushun. A Chinese patrol boat comes by, both trawlers leave at high speed pursued by the Chinese patrol boat. One of the North Korean Trawlers is blown up, the other escapes."

"The North Korean missile wasn't targeting China, so this can't have anything to do with it," JD said.

Kyle checked his laptop while Richardson ran the loop again.

"Our agency reports nothing in the Chinese news, or any other source," Kyle said. "What those two North Korean spy boats were doing up there, I can't explain. Their normal territory is down around South Korea and Japan."

Richardson put the real-time missile view back up on the screen. "Probably no connection to this missile launch. May have been some spy operation gone wrong, or just a mistake in the first place."

"Here's something," Kyle said. "Red Army Air Force in Manchuria, put on alert. A surveillance aircraft is in the air—that's normal—but two fighter wings on alert is not normal." Kyle looked at the faces around the table. "Whatever the North Koreans were trying to do with those trawlers upset the Chinese a good bit."

"We need to have that Global Hawk moved off the missile launch site and put on loiter over the west coast of Korea," Richardson said.

"The Chinese surveillance plane is flying regular patterns along their coast, and the fighters are still on the ground," Kyle said.

"One more thing, gentlemen," Richardson added. "Those two trawlers had a lot of active radar going, all aimed at the Chinese coast."

"Why?"

"Mapping the coast profile in detail."

"So?"

"We monitored their internal communications."

"You can do that?" JD said, surprised.

Kyle smiled the thinnest of smiles.

"Heard Russian being spoken, not just Korean," Richardson said.

Hallam came in and took his seat. Richardson

Rogue Patriot

briefed him that the SEALS were in the skimmer moving offshore to rendezvous with a submersible. "Should be in about twenty minutes, sir. Also request you ask that the Global Hawk be repositioned..."

A CID man took Hallam aside and began to speak urgently with him.

Kyle turned his laptop to Iselin. It showed waveforms unintelligible to JD.

"That spy boat that irritated the Chinese was using very high definition surface-scan radar. Mapping what the coastline of China would look like to an approaching ship."

"Why would the North Koreans want to have one of their ships approach the Chinese coast?"

"I don't know."

"From our intercept, make a visual profile of that highlighted area," Richardson told a petty officer.

"What the hell is a North Korean spy boat doing scanning the coast of China?" Hallam asked, obviously irritated. He cast a look at the departing CID man.

"Beats me, sir." Richardson looked at the papers in his hand. "Here's another puzzling item. They were using two boats, setting up line of sight, to lock in the position. Our folks use the same method. One boat was apparently having engine trouble and its skipper got chewed out by the lead boat, clear language Korean. No code."

"So?"

"In the background we heard two people speaking Russian."

Hallam studied the man. "Saying what?"

"Our translators couldn't really make it out, but the speakers had East Russian, Vladivostok, accents."

Hallam looked at the men around him. "Any speculation?"

Blank faces all around the table.

"You've got the ball on this one, David," Hallam told Kyle.

CHAPTER 12

The Operations Center had gotten quiet. A number of people had taken this opportunity to step outside for a break.

"Missile warhead is making its pass through the satellite zone, sir," A Navy Commander, young for his rank, with sand-colored hair and an uneasy look told Hallam and JD. "I'm Commander Marsten, sir. Rear Admiral Richardson is getting some rest."

"Which I need myself," Hallam told him. "Proceed."

"Yes, sir, the missile's first stage took it to 100,000 feet as designed, no anomalies in its ascent trajectory. But after it staged to the liquid second stage, it began a 5° cant to the northwest which could not be corrected during the three minute burn of the third stage. It is not in the stable orbit...."

"—Just tell me about the pass through the satellite belt before it re-enters atmosphere," Hallam interrupted.

"Yes, sir," The commander put up a global projection and used his red cursor to show the estimated track. "It's passing into this zone now, moving very fast. But if they trigger it in the next minute it could do some damage."

Everyone in the Op Center sat in exhausted silence watching as the yellow track passed through the satellite zone delineated in pale purple on the screen.

Nothing happened.

Hallam nodded. "Contact Space command and confirm there was no firing, no detonation."

"Take a look at this," JD handed Hallam the sheet Tomoko had written.

Admiral Hallam's face darkened. "This is reliable?"

JD nodded. "Lt. Commander Hare leaked info on this Op to the Koreans. Not intentionally, but they are familiar with your normal ship and aircraft routines. They could tell you were going to put Americans on the ground in North Korea. Didn't know how many since a tiltwing can carry up to twenty men."

There was a tightly controlled anger in Hallam's

voice now, "That's what the CID just briefed me on."

"Once the submersible gets past the coast horizon line and into international waters, we'll get a report from the SEALS." Marsten glanced at his watch. "But not for at least forty five minutes."

Hallam stood, "I'm going to the communications center to take my beating for authorizing this. But as soon as we have contact with the submersible, I want a quick after-action report from the men on the ground."

Hallam stood and rolled his shoulders, "David?"

Kyle closed his laptop. "North Korea is still quiet, although a company of Kim's elite palace guard is moving by truck to the ballistic missile launch site. This appears to confirm that Kim did not authorize the launch. No mobilization of ground troops in North Korea. But that is not true of South Korea, they are on full alert, their antiballistic missile net is still ranging around the road network, presumably in case there's a second launch."

"I need to talk to my bosses immediately," Hallam said on his way to the door. "Let them know what we've done, see if they can calm the South Koreans down."

The CID Lieutenant Commander approached.

"We've taken Lt. Commander Gary Hare into custody, sir. On suspicion of passing classified information to Japanese nationals who in turn passed it to North Korean agents."

Hallam's faced knotted. "I have to speak to the Secretary of Defense now. Keep the arrest of Lt. Commander Hare quiet. No in or out communication."

"Uniform Code of Military Justice allows legal counsel..."

"Nobody! Not until after I've spoken to the Secretary of Defense."

As Hallam passed, JD said softly, "You can tell them it was ISO..."

Hallam put his hand on JD's shoulder, "Doesn't matter what uniform the men who scrambled the missile wore, they acted under my orders. And as I told you I have no authorization from CINCPACFLT or anybody else."

"Best defense is a good offense," JD said. "Your initiative succeeded. They won't argue with success."

Hallam nodded. "I'll tell them the whole truth and hope our elected officials aren't so dumb as to publicly claim Americans interfered in a North Korean missile launch. If we say nothing, the North Koreans will save face and say it was a scientific mission that went

Rogue Patriot

off course, and things will stay calm."

The screen operator tiled-in news from a half dozen sources. "Here's what the world is talking about."

Pyongyang had still not made any official announcement about the missile launch. International news media had been caught off guard by the unannounced launch. Talking heads were speculating. The news services, both streaming and broadcast, ran endless loops of old footage of North Korean missile launches. American and South Korean officials were interviewed, but no one was producing any real information. The North Korean silence ignited speculation that the launch was the work of a 'rogue General,' which stimulated the beltway think tank spokespersons to start harping on how they had warned Washington months ago about unauthorized and unpredicted military activity on the Korean peninsula, and its potential to pull both the U.S. and China into conflict.

JD wandered out of the building into a warm afternoon. The silence was good. Another few hours until Flash would be back on base. *I've got a few minutes to relax.* He had just started down the long white sidewalk when his phone buzzed.

It was Admiral Hallam's aide. "The Admiral needs you in the secure communications center immediately."

CHAPTER 13

In the North Korean weapons development compound on the west coast of North Korea, Director Park Jae Soo sat in his office staring at the reports spread across his battered wooden desk. A Pine Tree cigarette smoldered in the overflowing ashtray. It was cold in his plywood cubicle in the coastal cave.

Park had been working almost continuously for ten days. The nuclear weapon he had designed was now installed on the Russian-made cruise missile that sat behind him on its rail car launcher, like a great prehistoric beast.

Exhaustion had driven Park's mind to dream. A familiar dream of white cherry blossoms, the cloud of white blossoms drifting down from the trees like snow. Children ran through the cloud, hands in the air, shrieking with delight. The March day was warm and bright.

That had been more than thirty years ago. In Tokyo's Ueno Park.

One of his assistants knocked on the frame of his office doorway. "General Chae is here." There was tension in his voice.

"Show him in and return to your desk." No guards preceded General Chae, a short muscular man in a red-piped blue army general's uniform. He smiled as he entered Park's cubical, showing perfect teeth. His teeth were legendary in North Korea. Like all powerful North Koreans, Chae went out of country for his dental work, while the rest of the populace suffered with third-rate dentists or none at all.

Park made no effort to straighten the civilian tunic he wore as a small symbol of his bit of independence from the military machine that was North Korea.

Chae stood in front of Park's desk. "So nice to see you again, Director Park," Chae said pleasantly.

Park stood and bowed. The young general indicated Park could sit. Park was offered a Marlboro, which he eagerly took, and they both lit up. Chae stood quietly for a moment, examining the wooden cubicle, the dark rock ceiling twenty meters overhead, the

Rogue Patriot

shadowy form of the cruise missile on its launcher. He blew smoke at the roof of the cave.

"Your family is well?" Chae asked. A shudder went through Park. That phrase was often the state police's indication that a person's family would be at risk if he did not cooperate.

Chae laughed, "I am not threatening you."

"Yes," Park said. He looked into the general's calm grey eyes, very rare in Koreans, eyes of such light color.

"You have no doubt wondered about all this." Chae's gesture took in the Russian missile on its launch car looming in the dim cave, the warhead fitted into its nose cone.

Park remained silent. It was never wise to volunteer information to the police or the military. "I'm sure you wondered why our operational nuclear warhead has been brought out of the secure production facility," Chae said, "without orders from Pyongyang, then driven down ordinary roads in an unmarked truck, to this cave." Chae smiled at Park's silence. "And why this missile was delivered here direct from the Russians at Vladivostok. Of course you wondered. But you were smart enough to follow my orders without asking for confirmation from Pyongyang."

Chae stamped out his half-smoked cigarette. Park was shocked at his wastefulness. Chae smiled. "I want that missile launched soon. Very soon. What use are tools if they are never used? Is the guidance calibration complete?"

"We do not have the coastal profile..."

"And you won't get it," Chae said. "Set the guidance to inertial only. There will be no terrain radar or global positioning confirmation."

He got up and paced a step or two each way.

"I am a patriot," Chae told Park in a conversational tone. "And that has always required a certain focus, a certain willingness to sacrifice, and the ability to improvise, to accomplish what is best for our people." Chae's pale eyes burned into Park's.

Threatened and exhausted, Park heard himself answer, "What have we gained if, in fighting imperialism, we become fascists instead of the socialists we say we are. The people's lives in our country will not improve..."

Chae stepped close to Park. "You know nothing of the people's lives. Only what you see out the train window. You have lived better than most of them." Chae carried a riding crop, ornamented with his family crest, a throwback to Japanese Imperial army

Rogue Patriot

regalia he admired. He touched Park's chest with it. "That pacemaker you wear, that is privilege. You live because of me. I arranged for all that. And I left you alone with your school children, to whom you could speak Japanese and think about the past."

Chae paced around the plywood cubicle. "You belong to me. From the expensive education my predecessor provided you, to this 'research' facility I provide you, to your comfortable house, servants, imported food and drink."

Chae lit another Marlboro with a gold Dunhill lighter and did not offer Park one. The desk lamp, in the gloomy unroofed cubicle, gave the two men's faces a cozy glow, a campfire on some pleasant excursion.

But Park knew he was listening to one of the most dangerous and unpredictable men in North Korea.

"Your little school," Chae continued. "Japanese nationals learning the glory of Korea's history so that when they are returned to Japan they can help Korea become as great as she once was."

Park rose. "I followed orders from the Information Ministry."

Chae blew smoke at the ceiling. "They are idiots. But I allowed you to keep your little school and the captured Japanese. Reeducating Japanese schoolgirls and sending them back to Japan is ridiculous. We don't want any Japanese in Korea, not even harmless children." Chae threw down another half smoked cigarette and Park fought the temptation to pick it up and smoke it.

"How long until we can launch?" Chae asked.

Park glanced at the grey shape on the launch car, beautiful in its symmetry, as most weapons were.

"Within the hour. My engineers are finished with the prelaunch testing now."

Chae smiled, "Then have some tea brought. We have an hour to enjoy each other's company."

Park called for tea.

"You were fortunate not to be involved in the Jang Sung-taek problems," General Chae continued.

"I have no interest in politics," Park answered honestly.

General Chae smiled sarcastically. "The failed nuclear detonation of 2006…only your friends at the ministry saved you. Very embarrassing for the son of a hero of the war against the Japanese."

Park said, "At your direction I have been special weapons director since 1994, the first days of the Kim Jong-un renaissance."

The tea was served and Chae drank a cup quickly.

"I know your career very well." He stood up. "I will not stay for the launch. I must return to Pyongyang to be there when the results of my efforts become clear." He brought his face close to Park's. "Do not fail. Two hours have passed since the Tae Po Dong launch. If that works as you have assured me it will, communications are now failing all over east Asia." Chae pulled out another cigarette and lit it.

"It is time for the next step. Launch this cruise missile at the target while I make my way to Pyongyang, where our great leader will soon need my help." Chae's handsome face twisted in anger. "The Han are the enemy. China is the empire to be feared, not Japan, not the U.S.A., not our brothers in the South."

"Launch the missile as soon as possible," he told Park. Then he turned on his heel and walked toward the rolling door, which was just opening.

He seemed a small figure marching toward his black car.

Park sat for a moment remembering cherry blossoms in springtime in Tokyo's Ueno Park. Then he roused himself and went out to see that launch preparations were proceeding smoothly.

CHAPTER 14

The atmosphere in the Ops Center had relaxed now that Flash and the two SEALS were out of North Korea and the Tae Po Dong 2 warhead had not caused any satellite damage. A depiction of the warhead re-entering atmosphere was now on the big screen.

JD stretched. Hallam sat slumped in his seat, clearly exhausted, but Richardson still hovered over him. JD could hear the conversation.

"Pyongyang's issued a statement, ambiguous this time, not bellicose like their usual posturing."

"Read it to me. No, put it up on the screen so everyone can see it."

It was short, took credit for a 'scientific' satellite launch and still managed to hint that foreign powers were responsible for the failure of a 'satellite' to orbit.

"Communiqué from South Korean Defense Forces, sir." An aide handed Hallam a paper. "South Korean anti-missile launchers are returning to their bases and other forces are standing down," Hallam read. An aide placed another note in front of Hallam.

"Space Command advises the North Korean 'satellite' did no damage to any orbital assets, military or commercial. The National Recon Organization says they will divert their Global Hawk to the North Korean West coast at our request, but can only stay on station twenty minutes due to fuel limits."

"Stay tied-in to the Global Hawk as it traverses to the west coast," Hallam said to his second in command.

"We seem to be through the worst of it sir," Richardson told him, "It may be a moot point now, but we still have the unanswered question of where the nuclear warhead went and why the North Koreans, or General Chae, moved it."

"Well," Hallam said. "You work it." Hallam stood and started for the door. "JD can I speak with you a moment?"

JD followed Hallam outside, where he was surprised to find it was already mid-afternoon. The sunshine felt good after hours in the Ops Center. The two men stood at the base of the steps of the Headquarters building, enjoying the sunshine.

"I had hoped to accomplish more in my career," Hallam told JD. "I should have said I wish I had accomplished more in my life. I gave up...certain things… to promote my career. That may have been a mistake."

Embarrassed at this revelation, JD said. "You just diverted a missile launch that could have been a catastrophe for the world economy. That's no small thing. Once the..."

"I only have a few weeks to live," Hallam interrupted, looking at the blue sky and the deep green lawn. "I have pancreatic cancer—stage four—incurable."

JD was aghast.

The glass door of the Headquarters building opened behind them and Richardson came down the steps, "Sir, sorry to intrude, but we have some intelligence we need to discuss."

"Give me a minute," Hallam told him, "Get David Kyle and we'll meet at the small conference table in the Ops Center."

Rogue Patriot

"You won't need me," JD said.

"We will need you," Hallam said. "We still need an outsider's viewpoint. Don't repeat what I just told you about my health." He turned a thin smile on Iselin. "And try not to be embarrassed by my revelation, though I know I would be if you were telling me the same things. I just needed to say these things out loud once, to ease my own mind. I chose you as confidante. Sorry for the imposition."

"It's no imposition," JD said, following him back into the artificial lights of the Operations Center.

Richardson spoke, "We don't know how Chae expected to capitalize on the communications blackout he tried to create. We also do not know why the North Korean's one operational nuclear warhead was moved or where it was moved. But the spy boat incident implies Chae had something in mind that relates to China."

"A communications blackout might simply have been a plan to slow down the growth of the Chinese economy, and ours too, while North Korea catches up," JD ventured.

"Not likely," Dave Kyle said. "Chae likes big dramatic moves. Simply slowing down our economies is not his psychology at all. He's after something more dramatic."

"If his shotgun blast had worked, we might have seen direct intervention by the western nations..."

"That's not likely," Hallam said. "We don't have the political will, the Japanese constitution prevents them from going on the offensive, and unlike us, they do abide by their own laws. South Korea, maybe, but not likely. And I don't think a communications blackout would be a big enough provocation for China to invade North Korea."

"China still has two fighter wings on alert but has made no other move, not even increasing their border patrol aircraft activity," Kyle reported. "That posture is consistent with their strategic planning in which they counter a ballistic missile with boost phase weapons."

"Here's a strange bit of info," Richardson said. "A low reliability report of North Koreans in Vladivostok buying weapons."

"They bought the guidance package for their Tae Po Dong 2 from Russia," Kyle said. "But not in Vladivostok. The guidance package was bought through Iran as usual."

"Here's something," Richardson said, paging through the reports, "Raduga. What's that a code name for?"

"What!" David Kyle was on his feet. "That's a Russian-made cruise missile. State of the art. And Chae wouldn't be able to get that through Iran."

CHAPTER 15

Richardson shook his head, "They've got their own anti-ship cruise missile, the Geun Seong..."

"Range is only fifty miles. Did our intelligence get any specs on which model Raduga the Koreans, Chae no doubt, bought?"

"Raduga IV, according to this."

Kyle shook his head, "Damn! A Raduga IV has an eight hundred kilometer mile range, 600-knot cruise speed, and is capable of carrying the North Koreans' heavy nuclear warhead. Damn!"

"So what target is Chae planning to take out under cover of a satellite blackout, using an 800 kilometer range cruise missile?" JD asked.

"Anywhere in Japan, Guam, Alaska..."

"The guidance package on a Raduga IV is inertial and TCM, no GPS."

"TCM?"

"Terrain contour matching," Kyle told him "Perfect for operating without satellite navigation." Kyle looked at the other three men. "That's what that coastal radar target was intended for. Chae now knows his communications blackout failed. But he's committed. Kim Jong-un will likely execute him for the unauthorized ballistic missile launch. So if Chae has a cruise missile he will launch it. He's got nothing to lose at this point."

The Intel chief was suddenly pacing, "So Chae's people were setting up a range target on the Chinese coast. As the cruise missile goes over, it calibrates on that point. From there on it matches inertial readings with terrain contour until it reaches its target."

"Chinese air defense won't even notice it until too late," Kyle said. "That cruise missile will be flying very low, over ocean, then over relatively unpopulated northeastern China."

"What's Chae's target with this thing?" Hallam asked, already knowing the answer.

"Knock out the Chinese leadership in Beijing and there'll be chaos in China. It's a highly centralized government."

Hallam was on his feet. "Richardson, have someone

get a polar projection map over here, thousand kilometer radius from any suspected cruise missile launch site on the northwest coast of North Korea."

When the freshly printed map was laid on the table Hallam took a straightedge and pencil and swept out an eight hundred kilometer radius circle.

"Beijing is the only logical target in that part of China," Kyle said.

"Jesus," JD breathed.

"Whether that missile is targeting Beijing or not, it needs to be stopped," Hallam said. "But unlike the ballistic missile, it can launch from any railroad track."

Kyle said, "The design bureau compound is on the west coast of Korea, far from South Korea and Japan, but still reasonably close to Pyongyang. And on a railroad track."

Hallam pointed at Richardson, "Get me some sea level digital reconstructions of the North Korean coast."

"A railroad goes right along the west coast of North Korea," Kyle continued. "Then it curves to the northeast to Vladivostok, Russia. Chae brought the cruise missile from Vladivostok by train directly to the nuclear design compound on the west coast of Korea. They moved a decoy warhead out of the design compound to make us think it was going to be fitted to the ballistic missile while they kept the real warhead in the design compound and fitted it to the cruise missile when it was delivered."

"How can we neutralize that cruise missile?" Hallam asked.

"Bomb the launch site," the Air Force Colonel stated. "We need to get bombers in the air immediately."

"No!" Hallam snapped. "Take too long. And even if it succeeded it would inflame everybody, China, South Korea, North Korea..."

Kyle looked at JD, "A cruise missile guidance can be scrambled with an EMP charge just as easily as a ballistic missile's."

The Marine Colonel shook his head. "The SEALS and your man who know how to operate drones are still on the submersible on their way back to Japan."

"We could fly a helicopter out to the submersible, retrieve the SEALs, fly them to the launch site," Richardson said hopefully. "At the launch site they could assault with small arms..."

"Still takes too long, " Hallam said. "And it would be suicide for whoever went in."

"Maybe not," Kyle added. "Chae's acting on his

own, keeping this secret. There won't be a bunch of troops around. It will be him and the weapons design team. They are scientists, not soldiers..."

A sailor came up with a sheet of paper with a computer generated image on it. "Got it." He laid the image on the map, and with a pencil indicated a small cove on the west coast of North Korea. "Ninety percent match to the depiction of the coast on radar?"

Kyle laid the straightedge between Beijing and the cove. "500 kilometers. Forty minutes flight time. We've got to do something—and do it now."

JD stared at the polar projection of North Korea and China someone had put on the big screen.

"I've got one more Ghost, a new model in secure storage," JD said slowly. "And I know how to fly it."

All eyes turned to JD.

JD returned the gaze.

Hallam said, "If you go to the airfield right now, fly straight to the launch site, and parachute in low, you can be there in less than an hour. I'll notify Air/Sea to airlift a sea skimmer to the area. After you've EMP'd the cruise missile, the skimmer will pick you up and move offshore, then submerge until I can get a ship there to retrieve it."

Hallam paused, his hand on the phone in front of

him. "But it is up to you. I can't order you to do this."

Just then Richardson was passed a note. "Sorry to interrupt, sir, but the ISO home office has been trying to reach Mr. Iselin for the last hour. They say it is extremely urgent." He handed the note to JD.

Repeat message: Please confirm you have had Navy destroy Ghost III. Signed Lori Turner, Chief Operating Officer, Iselin Security Options.

"Something important?" David Kyle asked.

JD crumpled the note. "No, nothing."

He straightened his shoulders. "Get me to the launch site. I'll scramble the missile's guidance with the Ghost III prototype if I can get near it undetected. The explosive charge in the Ghost III is very high yield. Everyone inside that cave will be shotgunned when it goes off. That will clear the way for me to get out to the sea skimmer."

Hallam rose and shook JD's hand.

CHAPTER 16

JD trotted to the practice field, got the Ghost III out of the security container, and carried it gingerly to the tiltwing. The aircraft lifted off as soon as he was on board. He checked the Ghost III's battery charge, and the simple control functions of the controller. He'd flown Ghosts before, but it had been six months, and even then, he was not nearly as proficient as Flash. This thing could blow up at any minute. Altitude change, a small impact, anything. He had been a pretty good skydiver; he liked freefall. But it had been a year since he'd made a jump.

"Time to get into your gear, sir," a petty officer third class told JD.

JD carefully set the box containing the Ghost aside. "Set my chute for the softest opening, OK?" It

Rogue Patriot

was awkward in the low cabin of the plane, but JD managed, with help, to get into his HALO coverall/parachute. He slipped the helmet on and tested the night vision in the red glow inside the aircraft. The audio and the video feed seemed to be working. He gave the thumbs up signal to the petty officer and slipped the helmet off.

"Where are your boots, sir?"

JD froze. "I don't have any." Both men stared at JD's Rockports in the red light of the cabin. "Use mine, sir," the petty officer slipped off one of his camo RDX boots, but it was two sizes too big. JD handed it back with a grin. "I'll have to attend this event a little underdressed for the occasion." He slapped the petty officer on the shoulder. "It's a walk in the park. I don't need fancy footgear."

The sailor adjusted JD's chute. "I'm setting it for a soft open and slow descent. You'll touch down light as a feather. Can't have you spraining an ankle on touchdown."

"What's the drop altitude?"

"Fifteen hundred feet."

The red numbers on the digital panel over the door lit up and started counting backward. "Two minutes," the sailor said unnecessarily. JD had the fold-up Ghost controller in his breast utility pocket over his ceramic armor. He had the Ghost itself rigged to the front of his coveralls. If it went off, he wouldn't feel a thing. If he touched down and rolled he might be able to soften the impact. Now I know how a suicide bomber feels, he thought, holding the Ghost to his belly.

"Get your helmet on sir," the sailor said. "Once the rear door opens I won't be able to hear you." JD slipped it on and adjusted volume. "Hear you loud and clear."

As the digital meter hit one minute the rear ramp began to let down. The rugged coastline was grey and dull green, the ocean a sheen of silver.

JD got to his feet and walked toward the ramp. He felt the aircraft slowing. The clock hit ten seconds. JD took four large steps forward and was out in freefall, arms and legs spread wide to stabilize. Within three seconds he reached terminal and the automated controls deployed his chute. Ten seconds later he'd settled into a bush, cradling his belly to protect the Ghost.

He lay there for sixty seconds listening, but nothing seemed to be moving anywhere near. He got to his knees, disconnected his chute, and unpacked the Ghost. He pulled the controller out of his pocket, and let the device find the navigation satellites it needed.

Rogue Patriot

He switched on the drone, let it rise up silently and move out over the little valley where the railroad tracks entered the missile storage cave.

The big rolling door to the cave was closed.

"Damn!" JD said softly. Global Hawk images from earlier this morning had showed it open. But at least they hadn't yet pushed the missile out along the railroad track.

He had counted on the rolling door being open.

Now what? He could wait, but the longer he waited, the more likely he'd be found, and the more likely they were to roll the missile out of the cave and fly it off.

He enlarged the video stream from the drone. Almost invisible in the overcast morning was the outline of a personnel door at the far left side of the rolling door. As JD watched, a Korean in civilian clothes stepped out and began pissing in the weeds near the railroad track.

JD put the drone on autonomous/follow and scrambled over the rocks, found a ravine and went down it fast to the bottom of the little valley, pulling out his pistol as he ran.

The Korean, oblivious to everything around him, was buttoning his pants up when JD shot him twice in the back with the silenced weapon.

JD ducked inside the door, ran the drone inside, and closed the door silently. He stood at the wall gasping for air while the drone rose silently to the rough ceiling of the cave. Large hanging lights lit a launcher-erector rail car and on it a Raduga cruise missile still painted Russian Strategic Rocket Forces grey with Cyrillic letters at the jet engine air intakes. A small diesel switching engine was stationed behind it to push the launcher out of the cave onto the railroad spur.

JD edged forward, crouching behind crates and worktables. He squatted and studied the overhead view the drone was giving him.

He could hear men talking from a makeshift set of control boards along one wall. Cubicles fabricated from plywood were hung with bare fluorescent tubes.

JD left the Ghost hovering at the ceiling and crept among the crates until he could get behind the switching engine, with a view of the men at the control boards. Three Koreans were at a jury-rigged control board immersed in their task. An older man JD recognized as Mr. Park and an assistant were at the missile's open control panel. The big steel tie-down transport straps had not yet been removed from the missile. They'd do that after they pushed it outside.

One of the Koreans disconnected several wires and closed the panel. He exchanged some words with Mr. Park that had the sound of finality. JD crouched behind the switching engine. Park returned to a chair at the control panel while two men pushed open the rolling door.

There was no indication they missed their colleague yet, or had noticed his body in the tall weeds beside the door. One man came purposefully toward where JD was hiding. JD slid under the switching engine. The gravel stunk of diesel fuel.

In the cab above him, the Korean guard switched on the starter engine, brought it up to RPM, and with a grind of gears engaged the diesel primary engine which chuffed over, belching blue smoke. It started with a roar and settled into a deafening idle directly over JD.

In his Ghost readout, JD could see the men at the control board. One sat, staring at the meters on the plywood panel, his hand near the switches on the desktop.

The man at the control board began to close switches. JD could see the glow changing from red to green. They were arming the warhead and engaging the guidance. Time to bring the Ghost down and detonate it.

A pair of boots dropped onto the gravel in front of JD's face. The engine driver shouted something to the men at the control panels then went back up into the cab.

I've got no time, JD thought. He flew the Ghost III down from the ceiling and smoothly along the missile to the control panel the men had just closed.

He pushed "enable," and when it had turned green, he pressed, "detonate" and the Ghost went off like the giant shotgun shell it was.

Shrapnel and flying gravel crackled around him, but flat on the ground nothing hit him. The men at the control panels had been riddled as though by shotgun fire. They slumped over their controls.

But the steel engine cab had protected the driver and when JD got to his feet the man fell on him from behind.

JD remembered enough of his hand-to-hand combat training to get a choke hold on him—two things were clear, he ate a lot of very sour kimchi, and he was not a soldier—but he fought back, hard.

The switching engine was in gear and was moving forward, slowly gaining speed, pushing the missile car out into the open. The turbojet began to spool up.

Rogue Patriot

JD pulled out his survival knife and threatened the man, who ran out the open door and disappeared into the brush beside the cave entrance.

JD ran down the rail spur ahead of the slow-moving missile.

A shot spanged off a rock near him. JD dodged to the other side of the missile car and trotted along beside it. *Using an armed missile for cover*, he thought as he ran. The turbojet was roaring, pushing the railcar faster.

This thing is trying to take off while it's still strapped to the rail car. I'm hiding behind an armed twenty kiloton nuclear weapon. He sprinted ahead of the rolling missile car, racing for the beach past the railroad tracks.

Behind him the missile on its car and the switching engine were picking up speed. JD glanced back. The air behind the jet engine was rippling with heat. JD activated his uplink button as he ran. "Get me out of here!" he gasped.

He leaped across the railroad tracks and slid down the embankment to the grey sand of the beach. It was empty, a hundred yards long, a rocky promontory at each end. Behind him, the missile on its rail car continued straight toward him.

The missile's turbojet was screaming, pushing the railcar launcher faster, but the tie-down straps held. The assembly ponderously reached the main railroad junction, then rumbled over the tracks. The switching engine decoupled; the launcher and the missile tilted down toward the dark sand of the beach.

A fireball went up as spilled jet fuel from ruptured tanks ignited.

JD reached the rocks at the North end of the cove and got behind one of them.

He realized his earbuds were beeping at him. "Iselin! Iselin! Do you read?"

JD pressed the throat microphone, "Yeah," he gasped.

"This is Kyle," David's normally calm voice was jittery with tension. "The Russians have an interlock on their cruise missiles. Even if the warhead is enabled, it won't go off until it leaves its launcher and reaches altitude."

"But there's no telling what burning jet fuel will do to the warhead igniters," JD told him.

JD caught sight of a sea skimmer coming into the cove, running full bore above water on its fans. JD stepped from behind the rock and waved his arms.

The skimmer came up onto the sand, fans

screaming, then pivoted, the ramp swung down, and two Marines jumped out and cinched a carry-lift around him. Then the three of them were jerked off their feet and reeled in as the skimmer accelerated for the ocean horizon.

JD pulled his helmet off and lay gasping on the deck. A Marine grinned down at him.

"Thanks, man," JD gasped.

The Marine nodded, "No trouble at all."

CHAPTER 17

The tiltwing settled onto the airfield with its customary jolt, and the big turbines started to spool down. JD, Flash, Callahan, and Seth wearily got to their feet, collected their gear, and filed out into the humid late afternoon.

Richardson and Kyle were there to meet them along with a crowd of sailors and marines. Callahan was ushered away by the men of the SEAL ground detachment.

"There's nothing I would like more than a shower and about ten hours sleep," JD told Flash. " But I can see that's not going to happen. You go get some rest then pick up all our gear and seal up that container for shipping home. Phone Lori and tell her I've done as she asked, destroyed the Ghost III."

Flash took off his cowboy hat, combed his dirty hair back with his fingers, and resettled it onto his head. "I'll get it done, but first I told Rick I'd meet him for a drink after we get cleaned up and he gets past his debrief. Eight o'clock at the CQB bar. Maybe you'd like to join us?"

JD shook his head, "Thanks, no."

Kyle pulled JD away. Soon JD, David Kyle, and Commander Richardson were lined up at a table in the secure communications room facing a TV screen with the Secretary of Defense, the President's aide for military affairs, and the Chairman of the Joint Chiefs of Staff appearing on it.

A side screen gave an overhead view of the outside of the missile cave in West Korea, still belching black smoke from a tangled ruin of machinery. It was surrounded, at a distance, by North Korean military vehicles of various sizes and types.

"Where's Admiral Hallam?" JD whispered to David Kyle as they settled into the black leather chairs. But the Secretary of Defense was already speaking.

"Mr. Iselin, your firm, and you personally, have rendered this nation a great service, and for that we are appreciative. But before you brief us, I caution you against discussing any details with anyone outside of

Naval Intelligence, is that clear?"

"Quite."

JD ran through the chain of events at the cruise missile launch site.

After the screen went blank, Kyle tilted his head, "Well, not as bad as it could have been."

JD stood up. "I've got to get cleaned up and get some rest, but I'd like to speak with Admiral Hallam first."

Richardson and Kyle traded glances. "I'm afraid that won't be possible, sir."

Richardson said, "Admiral Hallam is dead."

JD stared at the man.

"Apparent suicide, in his quarters, handgun. The Medical Officer tells me he was in the last stages of terminal pancreatic cancer—only weeks to live. I think he just decided to change the timetable a little."

JD wandered away and after a while found himself in the HQ building. Mrs. Suzuki let him into Hallam's office. Tomoko's two paintings still stood against the wall, but the family photo that had been the one decoration Hallam allowed himself was gone. He must have taken it with him to his quarters. JD remembered it distinctly. A young commander Hallam and his wife and daughter. It had been taken

Rogue Patriot

at Fisherman's Wharf in Monterey, California. JD knew the spot. He remembered Hallam had told him he'd spent a year there early in his career at the Naval Postgraduate School. "The happiest year of my life," he had called it.

JD closed the door and went out into the anteroom. Mrs. Suzuki stood. "I am pleased to see that you are alright," she said, bowing formally.

"Thank you."

"Do you know where I might find Tomoko?"

Mrs. Suzuki hesitated. "She has resigned. She will return to Matsue to live. Her hometown."

"I see," JD said. "If you speak with her, tell her thank you."

Mrs. Suzuki paused. "You might find her at Jagoshima at the Poet's Stone. She said she would go there now before leaving for Matsue."

"Thank you."

JD went out into the gathering dusk. There would be rain tonight. He had learned to tell from the clouds coming up Tokyo Bay.

He opened his phone and called Lori.

"Thank God you're alright!" she burst out. "We had rumors you were off on a mission and had taken Ghost III with you..."

"I was. It worked."

"You're lucky you survived. The tech guys have been working day and night—by the way—the money came in..."

"Lori, I'm dead tired, I can't think right now. Book me on the United flight from Narita to Chicago and on to DC tomorrow, will you? And expect a call from Flash. Book him on whatever flight he wants with a vacation enroute."

Ever efficient Lori said, "I'd recommend you take the American flight leaving tonight at nine. I'll get you first class so you can sleep..."

"Fine, fine," JD said, his eyelids drooping. "One more thing, would you consider being CEO of Iselin Security Options?"

There was silence on the line.

"Did you hear me, Lori?"

"Yes. Thank you, yes. I want your approval to..."

JD interrupted, "We can talk about all that later, whatever business is waiting for me, you do it." He clicked the phone off, but instead of going to his VOQ room, he went to the Main Gate.

The taxi let JD off at the top of a long flight of stairs that led to a spit of black sand beach. The five meter tall black granite poet's stone dominated the empty stretch of sand. Beside it stood a small figure in dark blue skirt and white blouse. JD told the taxi to wait and hurried down the stairs.

Tomoko.

"You don't need to leave Yokosuka," JD told her. "Lieutenant Commander Hare is gone. Your job is a good position with a good future…"

She watched the clouds coming in from Tokyo Bay in the dusk.

"The school in North Korea is gone," JD said. "The North Korean nuclear warhead melted down on the beach. That whole area is evacuated. The school house and that compound will be abandoned."

"They will build another one."

"What will you do in Matsue?" JD said.

The wind smelled of mist and the coming rain.

Tomoko said nothing.

Exhausted, JD only wanted to convince Tomoko not to run away, but he was too tired to think. "What is this?" JD asked, touching the polished face of the tall black stone.

"It is a poem," Tomoko said. "By a poet named Hakushu Kitahara. It is called 'Jagoshima Rain.'" Tomoko looked down at the black sand. "The poet is forgotten now."

"What is the poem about?"

"It is difficult to translate, but he says, things disappear from life, but the rain at Jagoshima does not change."

The mist was thickening toward a drizzle. "I will return to Matsue and live in my grandmother's house. Her ghost is still there waiting for me to return. She worries about me, because she lost me. I must help her ghost find the way."

He unfurled one of the cheap clear-vinyl umbrellas the taxi driver had given him. She unfurled her umbrella.

"I will live alone," she continued. "The little girl who was me disappeared and never came back. I am someone else now, a ghost of that girl." She gave JD a look that was both fierce and fearful. "I became another person when I was taken to Korea. While I was gone my grandmother died …" Her voice broke. "I must go now." She bowed to him and walked quickly toward the long stairs up to the street.

He stood at the base of the black stone and watched her make her way up the stairs.

After a while JD trudged up the stairs and had the taxi take him to Cheju Road, right outside the Navy base main gate.

Rogue Patriot

"Wait for me, please," he told the driver. The meter already showed he'd spent the yen equivalent of $120. But it was already eight o'clock and he needed to talk to Flash, and Callahan.

CHAPTER 18

The CQB bar was one of a row that stretched for two blocks, both sides of Cheju road, just outside the main gate of Yokosuka Navy base. Flash was on the center barstool, two SEALS on his left, a big bottle of OB beer open in front of him.

"How long have you been with ISO?" a SEAL asked Gordon.

Gordon laughed his engaging laugh, "Two years. But I've been a civilian for ten. Working the whole time. First Dyncorp, then I went with SAIC, left them when they got out of ops. Leidos, Scitor. But ISO's the best."

"Triple Canopy?"

Gordon straightened. "Once, long time ago. Blackwater too, for a year, way back in the day…"

Rogue Patriot

One of the SEALS at the pool table sauntered over to Gordon and stuck out his hand. They shook hands. "You've seen your share of the shit. What's it like going private?"

Callahan, at the pool table, laughed. "He's going to tell you how great it is. Don't believe him."

Flash laughed and raised his glass. "Every organization has its good points and its bad."

"I heard you flunked out of green team, when you first applied to SEAL training," Callahan said, but not in a critical tone.

"Lots of guys did," Gordon responded without rancor.

"Yeah," the guy taking aim on the nine-ball said with a laugh. "I did. Then came back and passed."

"Me too," Gordon said, unembarrassed. "Passed on my second try. Instructor there named O'Connell—he was smart, sharp, the best instructor I ever had—he told me to cool it for a year, think about whether I really wanted it or not, then come back. I did, and I passed, then spent ten years doing ops, including Trident Spear. When McRaven retired as chief of Southern Command, I retired."

Gordon ordered another beer. "I like working for Iselin. He's sharp, got the moves, knows how to schmooze the congressmen, keep the contracts coming. And his tech section is the best I've ever seen. We've got better equipment than you guys. No offense."

Callahan eyed Gordon. "Sometimes you sound like you think Iselin is hot shit, other times you think he's just a desk jockey. Which is it?"

"After what he did this week, you bet I think he's hot shit." Gordon finished his beer. A fresh one appeared on the bar.

"My treat," Callahan said. "But you're only as good as your last Op, right?"

"Always." Flash said. "But JD assures me he's going stay in DC from now on, no more field work. He's a good field man, but a better manager. ISO's success rate is the best I've seen of all the PMC's I've worked for and the casualty rate is the lowest."

"PMC?"

"Private Military Company. Wave of the future, guys. You'll all be working for one in ten years. You should get out of your Navy contracts now while you're still at the peak of your form. Get into the real world. Pay's better. And you can turn a job down if the OpPlan has been written by some moron who's never been in the field. On active duty, you have to just salute, say 'yes sir,' and go get shot."

Rogue Patriot

Callahan started to say something more, but Gordon wasn't finished, "Iselin's not a blame shifter. He'll take the heat if his own people screw up. We trust him and he trusts us." Flash drank some beer. "Years ago when the company was much smaller and he was doing a lot of field work himself, he saved my ass a time or two."

Ortega came over to get a fresh beer. "How long you got to sign up for?"

Callahan gave him a shove, "What are you doing, jumping ship?"

"Two year contracts," Gordon said, "But you can retire any time. No hassle, no stalling around, no cutting your retirement back. We all know when we're finished with field work. At the least the smart ones do." Gordon gave Callahan a look.

"Retirement any good?"

"Better than yours. Better buy your condo in Thailand now. You won't be able to afford it later."

"Why should we quit the Navy?" a guy at the pool table called over to Gordon. "We love the Navy." Everybody laughed.

"Sure," Flash conceded. "But the Navy is going to be using PMC's a lot more in the future. To bulk up for a specific op, so they can tell Congress their manpower levels are lean and mean."

"Mercenaries' loyalty is to money, not the U.S.A.," the guy shooting pool with Ortega said. He said it lightly but all the SEALS were listening for Gordon's response.

"Loyalty?" Gordon laughed. "CID just hauled off one of your Navy clods, for spying. So don't tell me about loyalty."

Gordon eased back against the bar and tipped his beer.

At the front door a couple of the SEALS were blocking a guy from coming in.

"Our bar, man. Off limits to you. Lots of other bars down the block."

Callahan caught a glimpse of the guy. He was an American, wearing a suit, no tie.

"Let him in," Callahan called. He sauntered over "Hello, JD. Looking for someone?"

Iselin nodded. "Yeah. You."

"Step into my office, then," Callahan said, steering him to the bar. Beers appeared.

"Hello, Flash," Iselin nodded at Gordon. Iselin touched the brown beer bottle in front of him. "I'm going back to the States tomorrow," Iselin told Callahan. "But thought I'd..." his words trailed off.

Rogue Patriot

He looked around the neon blue and red of the room, at the ceiling, at the beer bottle in his hand. "I don't know…I guess maybe I just wanted to say thanks."

Callahan exchanged glances with Gordon.

"And to let you guys know something else," JD continued.

"We've heard about Hare," Callahan said quietly. "The spy."

"Yeah, a lying little traitor," one of the SEALs said.

"CID tells me he is threatening to file a counter-suit against the Navy," JD said. "He's accusing Hallam of disobeying orders, initiating an illegal action. And Lt. Commander Hare was the only one trying to stop him." JD smiled. "His defense also includes an accusation of inappropriate use of contractors like Flash and me."

Flash raised his beer in a mock toast.

JD studied his beer for a moment. "But it won't do him any good. Admiral Hallam is dead." Faces turned to Iselin. The SEALS at the pool table stopped their game. The sound system kept playing 60s oldies, but the room seemed silent.

"Hallam had terminal cancer it seems," JD went on. "Medics found him dead in his quarters this evening." Iselin took a sip of beer. "Used his father's old service automatic to speed up the dying process a little. The Navy will bury him with honors. They'll minimize our little escapade; focus instead on a couple of North Korean technological breakdowns. That's what our government wants, that's what the Chinese government wants." Iselin took a long drink of his beer. Flash and the SEALs gathered around.

"But regardless of what you hear the news wonks saying, I am here to tell you Hallam was a patriot in the truest sense of the word. He had courage and was willing to take the initiative for what the constitution of the United States stands for. So I came here to honor him, with the only people who understand what patriotism really is."

Bottles of beer were served. No one spoke.

JD raised his beer. "To Admiral William Hallam the third, patriot." They all drank.

Callahan waved the bartender over, but Iselin shook his head. "No. Got to be on my way. Just wanted to tell you that Hallam was gone. And to say thanks."

He shook hands with Callahan and with Flash, then walked out into the crowds and neon glow of Cheju road to take his taxi to the airport.

CHAPTER 19

JD sat in one of the mini office cubicles in the United Airlines Royal Lounge. His flight to Washington DC would board in thirty minutes. "One more," he told the waitress, holding up his empty Jameson's glass.

Admiral William Hallam loved America, but hated what she had become.

JD knew he should be reviewing the task order for more Ghosts but instead ordered a Jameson whiskey neat and read email, message boards, news. The news was all about the failure of a North Korean ICBM launch and the melt-down of a North Korean nuclear warhead. The stories in the commercial news media were wildly inaccurate, contradictory, and repetitive. Newsmen interviewed anyone who would stand still and they all had opinions, most of them uninformed.

There were endless loops of stock footage of Kim Jong-un, most of it very old.

Nearly all the military message traffic JD saw was highly laudatory of Hallam—the man tough enough to take out a cruise missile without getting us in a shooting war with the Chinese.

The official Japanese statements were all very complimentary of America's willingness to stand behind her treaties to help defend Japan. A couple of people at the Naval Post Graduate School called Hallam a true hero, a man willing to take chances for the right cause.

One academic called him a rogue. The talking heads soon had that label bannered on all the channels 'Admiral William Hallam: A Rogue Patriot'. That made JD smile. *Hallam's a hero. But if his plan had failed, and it nearly did, twice, Beijing would be radioactive dust, The enraged Red Army would send tanks to overrun North Korea and South Korea, and the U.S.A. would be in a land war on the Korean peninsula that we could not win.*

For career military men and women, there has always been a very fine line between bold initiative and career suicide. For every failed mission, a scapegoat will be found. Somebody's got to hang.

Rogue Patriot

JD stared at his drink. "Well…Ghosts work. We've field tested them." He looked at the preliminary purchase order from Navy that would triple ISO's cash flow. But he felt no elation. "We need to ramp up production. Southern Command is already squawking about needing a dozen immediately."

Iselin stared at his empty glass thinking about what lay at the other end of this eighteen-hour flight.

The answer was: nothing. His bleak rooms at Homewood Suites in Crystal City, fourteen-hour workdays, restaurant tables for one, coming home to an empty apartment. Nothing.

The waitress's shadow was outside the frosted glass of the mini-office. *I'll have another Jameson's. Maybe that'll help me get through the review of the terms of this emergency sole source requisition.*

The door slid open, and there was Cheryl. They looked at each other for a moment.

"Mind if I join you?" she asked. She looked good, tailored blue suit and red blouse.

"This is a surprise," JD said, rising. "What are you doing at the Tokyo airport?" He trailed the question off, realizing he might not want to know the answer.

"I came to see you," she said. She sat down in the micro-office and put her hands on the table.

"You flew to Japan to see me?"

"Yes," Cheryl said. "You've got a ticket in your pocket for your flight back to Washington, right? And it's a DOD no-penalty-for-changes ticket, right? You could change it, delay your arrival in Washington a week." JD nodded. Cheryl took two tickets out of her purse. "On the other hand, these tickets are non-refundable, non-changeable."

She laid the packet on the table—two tickets from Tokyo to Honolulu.

When he looked up at her, she raised her eyebrows in an unspoken question.

He nodded. "Yes." He touched her hand. "I've made Lori CEO. She can take care of this task order." JD put the task order back in his brief case. "There is one thing, Cheryl, I've got to confess. I used our house equity..."

Cheryl put her finger on his lips. "I know, Lori called me. Your baby, ISO, is debt-free again. I'm not in the least worried about the house equity, we can refinance, or sell the place. Lori also got me on a plane to Tokyo within two hours and made reservations for luxury accommodations in Honolulu for us."

JD smiled, and realized it was the first real, relaxed

Rogue Patriot

smile, that had crossed his face in far too long. "Yes, Lori's a gem. She'll make a good CEO. There's one other thing," JD said. He put his arms around her and kissed her. "I'm finished with field work. Time I stayed closer to home; time I spent more time with you."

Cheryl's smile was scintillating. "You've done your time in the field." She pulled back to get a better look at his face. And JD kept thinking, *she is beautiful, smart, understanding. How could I have wanted a divorce?*

"Some of the news people are calling you a real patriot," Cheryl told him.

"Some of them call me a mercenary," he said with a grin. "But as a smart man once told me, patriotism is not about labels, about getting your name in the news, not about parades, medals, or awards, and certainly not about money, which is all that motivates mercenaries, right? Patriotism is only about ideals. And those ideals are demonstrated only by our actions, not by anything else."

The flight departed on time and Cheryl quickly dozed off as the sun set. JD looked out at the darkness, thinking.

He took out the envelope the CID men had found in Admiral Hallam's quarters after his suicide. The opened envelope was stamped with the CID official investigation stamp but it was addressed to JD Iselin.

Hello JD,

Thanks for being the confidante and supporter I needed at a crucial hour. I'll be dead by the time you read this. I've had cancer for nearly two years now and the end was near, so I decided to select my own time for departure, but decided to leave you this short note of explanation. (My former students at the Naval Postgraduate School would laugh at my delivering one more lecture even though I am already dead.)

In 1986, I was a young commander, proud to be part of the support team for the SALT II negotiations in Reykjavik. It was the last one of a series of nuclear warhead reduction meetings between President Reagan and Mr. Gorbachev, and the negotiations were tough. The U.S. and U.S.S.R. seemed to be at parity and neither side wanted to give an inch. Then President Reagan unveiled his SDI 'Star Wars' missile defense system, and that was a bet the Soviets could not match. They folded, and at that moment, the Cold War was finally and permanently ended, without loss of a single life.

I have never forgotten those negotiations, or my realization that one determined man can alter the course of history for the better.

When I found I had only months to live, I knew I had to try to make a change that would leave things better than I found them. I believe I have. There is now a solid chance for direct U.S.- China military negotiations and a clear reason for doing so. We all see the instability of the North Korean regime, and the potential havoc they can cause as their weapons skills improve.

Challenges lie ahead. But that is always true, and I believe others will step forward in their turn and make their contributions.

It's been a privilege to know you and work with you. I won't thank you for your patriotism because I believe patriotism is its own reward.

Admiral William T. Hallam III, U.S. Navy

CPSIA information can be obtained
at www.ICGtesting.com
Printed in the USA
FFOW01n0030150416
23142FF